A DOUBTFUL ALIBI

"I got up to pour another drink. Our glasses are very big. I sat down again in the chair, whiskey in hand. And that, Inspector, is how I fell asleep. It's true. If it happened while I was asleep, I didn't hear a thing. A pain in my side woke me up. Finally, I started to go upstairs. I opened Christine's door out of habit. That's when I saw her as you did this morning."

The body had been found half out of bed, head hanging over a rug spotted with blood. Doctor Paul had counted twenty-one wounds inflicted by what the report called a sharp instrument . . .

Other Inspector Maigret Mysteries by
Georges Simenon

MAIGRET ON THE DEFENSIVE

Coming Soon from Avon Books

MAIGRET IN COURT
MAIGRET AND THE GANGSTERS
MAIGRET'S MEMOIRS
MAIGRET'S WAR OF NERVES

MAIGRET
HAS DOUBTS

GEORGES SIMENON

Translated from the French
by Lyn Moir

AVON
PUBLISHERS OF BARD, CAMELOT, DISCUS AND FLARE BOOKS

AVON BOOKS
A division of
The Hearst Corporation
105 Madison Avenue
New York, New York 10016

Contents

One

Madame Pardon's
Rice Pudding

The maid had just placed the rice pudding on the circular table, and Maigret had to make an effort to appear both surprised and gratified, while Madame Pardon, blushing, gave him a sharp look.

This was the forty-fourth rice pudding in the four years that the Maigrets had dined regularly once a month at the Pardons'. The Pardons in turn came once a month to Boulevard Richard-Lenoir, where it was up to Madame Maigret to provide a good meal.

Five or six months after the visits had started, Madame Pardon had served a rice pudding. Maigret had had three helpings, saying that it reminded him of his childhood and that for forty years he hadn't eaten one as good, which was true.

After that, every dinner at the Pardons' new apartment on Boulevard Voltaire finished with the same creamy pudding that underlined the character of these get-togethers—sweet, soothing, and a little dull.

Since neither Maigret nor his wife had any family in Paris, they had practically no experience of those evenings spent on a fixed day with sisters or sisters-in-law, and the dinners with the Pardons reminded them of childhood visits to aunts and uncles.

This evening the Pardons' daughter Alice, whom they had known as a schoolgirl and who had been married a year ago, was at the dinner with her husband. She was seven months pregnant and had the "mask of pregnancy," particularly the red blotches on her nose and under her eyes, and her young husband watched her diet carefully.

Maigret was going to say once again how delicious his hostess's rice pudding was when the phone rang for the third time since the soup. They were used to it. It had become a kind of game at the beginning of the meal to guess if the doctor would get to the dessert without being called by one of his patients.

The telephone stood on a wall shelf with a mirror above it. Pardon, napkin in hand, grabbed the receiver.

"Hello, Doctor Pardon . . ."

The others were silent, watching him, when suddenly they heard a voice so shrill that it made the phone vibrate. No one except the doctor could make out the words. They were only sounds piled one after the other, like a record played too fast.

Maigret, however, frowned as he saw his friend's face become grave, a worried look spreading over it.

"Yes . . . I'm listening, Madame Kruger. . . . Yes."

The woman at the other end of the line needed no encouraging. The sounds fell over each other like a litany, incomprehensible but pathetic to those who didn't have their ear to the receiver.

A wordless drama was being acted out in the slight variations of expression on Pardon's face. The doctor, who had been watching the byplay with the pudding a few minutes before, now seemed to be far away from the quiet middle-class dining room.

"I understand, Madame Kruger. . . . Yes, I know. . . . If it would help you, I'll come and . . ."

Madame Pardon threw a look at the Maigrets that said, "See! Another dinner to be finished without him."

She was wrong. The voice shrilled on. The doctor grew more uneasy.

"Yes. . . . Of course. . . . Try to put them to bed. . . ."

They could see that he felt discouraged and helpless.

"I know. I know. . . . I can do no more than you can."

No one was eating. No one in the room spoke.

"You understand that if this goes on it's you who . . ."

He sighed and wiped his forehead with his hand. At forty-five, he was almost bald.

He finished by sighing wearily, as if he were giving in to unbearable pressure:

"Then give him a pink pill. . . . No, only one. . . . If that hasn't had any effect in half an hour . . ."

Everyone sensed a certain relief in the voice coming over the phone.

"I won't leave the house. . . . Good night, Madame Kruger."

He hung up and sat down again. The others avoided asking him what it was all about. It took several minutes to get the conversation going again; Pardon took no part in it. The evening kept to its traditional rhythm. They got up from the table and had their coffee in the living room, its table covered with magazines because that room was used as the waiting room during office hours.

Both windows were open. It was May. The evening was warm and the air of Paris had quite a springlike feel, in spite of the buses and the cars. Families were out strolling on Boulevard Voltaire, and there were two men in shirt sleeves on the terrace of the café across the street.

Cups filled, the women took up their knitting in their usual corner. Pardon and Maigret sat by one of the windows, while Alice's husband didn't really know which group to join and ended up sitting beside his wife.

It had already been decided that Madame Maigret would be the child's godmother, and she was knitting a little jacket for it.

Pardon lit a cigar. Maigret filled his pipe. They didn't particularly feel like talking, and quite a while went by in silence broken only by the hum of the women's voices.

The doctor finally spoke in a low voice, almost to himself:

"It's one of those evenings when I wish I'd chosen another profession."

Maigret didn't press him, didn't urge him to speak. He liked Pardon. He felt he was a real man, in the full sense of the word.

The other glanced at his watch.

"This could go on for three or four hours, but she might ring any minute."

He went on without giving any details, so that Maigret had to pick up the sense for himself:

"A tailor in a small way, a Polish Jew, living on
Rue Popincourt above an herbalists' . . . Five children, the eldest only nine, and the wife pregnant with
the sixth . . ."

He shot an involuntary look at his daughter's in-
creasing girth.

"No drug so far discovered can save his life, and
he has been on the point of death for five weeks. I've
done all I can to get him to go to the hospital. As
soon as I mention it he gets into a terrible state, calls
his family to him, weeps, groans, begs them not to
let him be carried off. . . ."

Pardon was finding no pleasure in his one cigar of
the day.

"They live in two rooms. . . . The kids cry. . . .
The wife's at the end of her tether. . . . She's the
one I ought to be taking care of, but as long as this
goes on there's nothing I can do. I went there before
dinner. I gave the man an injection and his wife a
sedative. They have no effect on them any more.
While we were at dinner he began to groan again,
then to shriek with pain, and his wife, with no strength
left . . ."

Maigret pulled on his pipe and murmured:

"I think I've got the picture."

"Legally, medically, I haven't the right to pre-
scribe another dose. This isn't the first telephone call
like that. Up until now I've managed to convince
her . . ."

He looked pleadingly at the Inspector.

"Put yourself in my place."

He glanced at his watch again. How much longer
would the sick man fight on?

The evening was soft, with a trace of mugginess in the air. The wives were still chatting in low voices in a corner of the room, their knitting needles marking the rhythm of the conversation.

Maigret said hesitantly, "It's not quite the same sort of case, of course. Sometimes I, too, have wished I had chosen another profession."

It wasn't a real conversation, with the dialogue following a logical pattern. There were gaps, silences, slow puffs of smoke rising from the Inspector's pipe.

"For some time now we policemen haven't had the powers we used to have, nor, therefore, the responsibilities."

He was thinking aloud and felt very close to Pardon, a feeling that was shared by the other man.

"In the course of my career I've seen our responsibilities shrink, while the magistrates have taken over more and more. I don't know if it's a good thing or not. In any case, we've never had to pass judgment. It's the job of the courts and the juries to decide whether or not a man is guilty and to what extent he is responsible."

He kept on talking because he felt that his friend was tense, his mind elsewhere, in the two rooms on Rue Popincourt where the Polish tailor was dying.

"Even with the law as it is at present, though we are only the instruments of the Public Prosecutor's Office and of the Examining Magistrate, there is still a moment when we have to take a decision on which a lot depends. Because, after all, the magistrates, and the juries eventually, form their opinions on the basis of our investigations, on the basis of the facts we have gathered.

"Just to treat a man as a suspect, to take him to Quai des Orfèvres, to question his family, his friends, his concierge, and his neighbors about him can change the entire course of his life."

It was Pardon's turn to murmur, "I understand."

"Was a certain person capable of committing a certain crime? Whatever happens, it is almost always we who have to be the first to ask ourselves that question. Material evidence is often nonexistent or hardly convincing."

The telephone rang. Pardon seemed afraid to answer it, and it was his daughter who picked up the receiver.

"Yes, monsieur. . . . No, monsieur. . . . No. . . . You have the wrong number. . . ."

Smiling, she explained to the others. "The Bal des Vertus again."

A dance hall on Rue du Chemin-Vert whose telephone number was similar to that of the Pardons.

Maigret went on in a subdued voice.

"This man facing you, who seems so normal, could he have killed someone? Do you see what I mean, Pardon? All right, so it's not a matter of deciding whether he is guilty or not. That's not the business of Central Police Headquarters. But we still have to ask ourselves *if it is possible*. And that's a kind of judging! I hate that. If that had occurred to me when I joined the force, I'm not sure if . . ."

A longer silence. He emptied his pipe and took another from his pocket, filling it slowly, seeming to caress the bowl.

"I remember one case, not so long ago . . . Did you follow the Josset case?"

"The name rings a bell."

"It had a lot of publicity in the papers, but the truth, if truth there was, has never been told."

It was rare for him to talk of a case in which he had taken part. Sometimes, on Quai des Orfèvres, among themselves, they would mention a well-known case or a difficult investigation, but it was always just a few words.

"I can see Josset at the end of his first interrogation, since that was when I had to ask myself the question. I could let you read the report and see what you think. But you wouldn't have had the man in front of you for two hours. You wouldn't have heard his voice, watched his face and expressions."

The place was Maigret's office on Quai des Orfèvres; the day, he remembered, was a Tuesday, the time about three in the afternoon. And it was spring then, too, the end of April or the beginning of May.

When the Inspector arrived at the Quai that morning he had heard nothing about the case, and he was only called at ten o'clock, first by the Inspector at the Auteuil police station, then by Coméliau, the Examining Magistrate.

There was some confusion about everything that day. The Auteuil police claimed that they had informed Police Headquarters in the early hours of the morning, but for one reason or another it didn't appear that the message got through.

It was nearly eleven when Maigret climbed out of his car on Rue Lopert, two or three hundred meters from the parish church of Auteuil, and he found himself to be the very last. The reporters and photographers were there, surrounded by about a hundred spectators held back by policemen. The men from the Public Prosecutor's Office were already on the spot, and those from the Criminal Identity Division arrived five minutes later.

At 12:10 the Inspector ushered Adrien Josset into his office. He was a handsome man of about forty, only just beginning to put on weight, and, in spite of being unshaven and wearing rather crumpled clothes, he was still elegant.

"Please come in. Sit down."

He opened the door of the detectives' office and called young Lapointe.

"Bring a pad and a pencil."

The office was bathed in sunlight, and the sounds of Paris filtered in through the open window. Lapointe, who had understood that he was to take down the interrogation in shorthand, seated himself at one corner of the table. Maigret filled his pipe and watched a row of barges going up the Seine while a man in a small boat kept out of their way.

"I'm sorry, Monsieur Josset, but I have to note down your answers. You aren't too tired, are you?"

The man indicated that he was not with a slightly bitter smile. He had not slept the previous night and the Auteuil police had already questioned him at length.

Maigret did not wish to read their report, preferring to make his own judgment.

"Let's begin with the usual questions of identity— surname, Christian names, age, profession . . ."

"Adrien Josset, age forty, born in Sète in the Hérault region . . ."

One would have had to know that to pick out the slight accent of the Midi.

"What does your father do?"

"He was a primary-school teacher. He died ten years ago."

"Is your mother still alive?"

"Yes. She still lives in the same little house in Sète."

"Did you take your degree in Paris?"

"In Montpellier."

"I take it you are a pharmacist."

"I took my degree as a pharmacist and went on for a year with medical studies, but there I stopped."

"Why?"

He hesitated, and Maigret saw that it was from a kind of honesty. One could sense that he was trying very hard to answer correctly, truthfully, up to now at any rate.

"There were probably several reasons. The most obvious is that I had a girlfriend who went to Paris with her family."

"Did you marry her?"

"No. In fact we broke it off a few months later. I think, too, that I felt I wasn't cut out to be a doctor. . . . My parents weren't well off. They had to deprive themselves to pay for my studies. . . . And then when I qualified I would have had difficulty getting into a practice. . . ."

Because of his tiredness it was hard for him to follow his own train of thought, and he sometimes looked at Maigret as if to reassure himself that the Inspector understood him.

"Is that important?"

"Everything may be important."

"I see. I wonder if I ever had a real vocation. . . . I had heard of jobs being offered in laboratories—most big drug companies have research laboratories. When I got to Paris, diploma in hand, I tried to get one of those jobs."

"Without success?"

"All I found was a substitute post in a drugstore, then another."

He was hot. So was Maigret, who was walking up and down the room, stopping from time to time in front of the window.

"Did they ask you these things at Auteuil?"

"No. Different things. I can see that you're trying to find out what kind of person I am. As you see, I'm trying to answer you truthfully. I suppose that basically I'm no better and no worse than anybody else."

He mopped his brow.

"Are you thirsty?"

"A bit."

Maigret opened the door of the detectives' room.

"Janvier! Get us something to drink."

He turned to Josset.

"Beer?"

"That's fine."

"Aren't you hungry?"

Without waiting for an answer he went on, to Janvier:

"Beer and some sandwiches, please."

Josset gave a sad smile.

"I've read about that," he murmured.

"Read about what?"

"Beer, sandwiches. The Inspector and the detectives taking turns asking questions. It's common knowledge, isn't it? I never thought that one day . . ."

He had delicate hands that from time to time betrayed his nervousness.

"A person knows what it means when he comes in here, but . . ."

"Calm yourself, Monsieur Josset. I can tell you now that I have no preconceived ideas about you."

"The detective at Auteuil did."

"Was he rough with you?"

"Fairly rough. He used some words that . . . Never mind! Maybe in his place I would . . ."

"Let's go back to your first days in Paris. How long was it before you met the woman you eventually married?"

"About a year. I was twenty-five and working in an English drugstore on Rue du Faubourg Saint-Honoré when I met her."

"Was she a customer?"

"Yes."

"What was her maiden name?"

"Fontane. Christine Fontane. But she was still using the name of her former husband, who had died a few months before. Lowell, part of the English brewery family. You must have seen that name on bottles."

"So she had been a widow for several months. How old was she?"

"Twenty-nine."

"No children?"

"No."

"Rich?"

"Very. She was one of the best customers of the fashionable shops on Faubourg Saint-Honoré."

"And you became her lover?"

"She led a very free life."

"Even when her husband was alive?"

"I have reason to think so."

"What kind of family did she come from?"

"Middle-class. Not rich, but comfortably off. She had spent her childhood in the Sixteenth Arrondissement, and her father was a director on the boards of several companies."

"You fell in love with her?"

"Very quickly, yes."

"Had you already broken off with your friend from Montpellier?"

"Several months before."

"Did the question of marriage between Christine Lowell and you come up right away?"

He hesitated only a second.

"No."

There was a knock at the door. It was the waiter from the Brasserie Dauphine, carrying beer and sandwiches. That made a break. Josset didn't eat, but he drank half his beer while Maigret marched back and forth munching a sandwich.

"Can you tell me how it came about?"

"I'll try. It's not easy. It was fifteen years ago. I was young, I see that now. Looking back, I think life was different then. Things weren't as important as they are now.

"I was earning very little. I lived in a furnished

room near Place des Ternes, and I ate in cheap restaurants when I could afford more than croissants. I spent more on clothes than I did on food.''

He had kept his taste for clothes, and the suit he was wearing came from one of the best tailors in Paris. His monogrammed shirt had been made to measure, as had his shoes.

''Christine lived in a different world, one which I didn't know and which dazzled me. I was still a provincial boy, a teacher's son, and in Montpellier my student friends were hardly any better off than I was.''

''Did she introduce you to her friends?''

''Only much later. There was one thing about our relationship that I didn't notice at the time.''

''What was that?''

''One often speaks of businessmen, industrialists, or financiers having an affair with a salesgirl or a model. It was a bit like that for her, the other way around. She made dates with a poor, inexperienced pharmacist's assistant. She had to know where I lived—it was a cheap hotel, the walls of the staircase were tiled. You could hear everything through the walls. She loved it. On Sundays she drove me to an inn in the country . . .''

His voice had grown duller, tinged both with nostalgia and with a little resentment.

''At first I too thought it was just one of those affairs that wouldn't last.''

''Were you in love with her?''

''I grew to love her.''

''Were you jealous?''

''That's how it all started. She used to tell me

about her boyfriends and even about her lovers. She found it amusing to give me details. At first I said nothing. Then, in a fit of jealousy, I called her every name under the sun and ended up by hitting her. I was sure she was laughing at me behind my back and that when she left my little iron bed she went away to tell other men about my awkwardness and ingenuousness. We had several quarrels like that. I went without seeing her for a month."

"Was it she who came back?"

"She or I. One of us always asked to be forgiven. We were really in love, Inspector."

"Who first spoke of marriage?"

"I don't know. Frankly, I couldn't say. We got to the point where we hurt each other on purpose. Sometimes she knocked at my door, half-drunk, at 3 A.M. If I was sulking and didn't answer at once, the neighbors complained of the noise. I can't count the times they threatened to throw me out—at the pharmacy, too, I was late and half-asleep several mornings."

"Did she drink a lot?"

"We both did. I don't know why. It was a habit. The affair excited us too much. Finally we realized that I couldn't live without her and she couldn't live without me."

"Where did she live at that time?"

"In the house you saw, on Rue Lopert. It was about two or three o'clock one morning, in a night club, that we looked into each other's eyes and suddenly sobered up and asked ourselves seriously what we were going to do."

"Don't you know who asked the question?"

"Frankly, no. For the first time someone had mentioned the word 'marriage,' at first as a joke, or almost. It's hard to say when it was so long ago.''

''She was five years older than you?''

✗ ''And several millions richer. Once married to her I couldn't go on working behind the counter of a drugstore. She knew a man, Virieu, who had been left a small drug company by his parents. Virieu wasn't a pharmacist. He was thirty-five and had spent his life flitting between Fouquet's, Maxim's, and the casino in Deauville. Christine put some money into the Virieu company and I became the head of it.''

✗ ''So in fact you were achieving your ambition?''

''It looks like that, I know. If one looks back on the sequence of events, it does look as if I must have prepared each step carefully. In spite of that, I can tell you it's not true at all.

''I married Christine because I was passionately in love with her, and if I had had to leave her I would definitely have committed suicide. She in turn begged me to live legally with her.

''There was a long period when she had no more affairs and it was her turn to be jealous. She began to hate the customers at the pharmacy and came to spy on me.

''A chance came up that would give me a job commensurate with her style of living. The money put into the business stayed in her name, and the marriage was legally one of separate maintenance.

''Some people took me for a gigolo, and I haven't always been well received in the new society I had to live in from then on.''

''Were you happy together?''

''I think so. I worked hard. The laboratories used

to be little known, but now they're among the four biggest in Paris. We went out a lot, too, so there weren't any gaps, so to speak, in either my days or my nights.''

''Don't you want anything to eat?''

''I'm not hungry. Perhaps I might have another glass of beer?''

''Were you drunk last night?''

''That's what they asked me about most this morning. I must have been at one point, but my memory isn't any the less clear for it.''

''I didn't want to read the statement you made at Auteuil, which I have here.''

Maigret flicked over the pages carelessly.

''Would you like to change any of it?''

''I told the truth, perhaps in rather strong language because of the detective's attitude. As soon as he started to question me, I realized that he thought I was a murderer. Later, when the men from the Public Prosecutor's Office came to Rue Lopert, I felt that the Magistrate had the same idea.''

He was silent for a few moments.

''I can see their point. I was wrong to get angry.''

Maigret murmured, without too much stress:

''You didn't kill your wife?''

And Josset shook his head. He no longer made his protest angrily. He seemed tired and despondent.

''I know it's hard to explain.''

''Would you like to lie down for a while?''

The man hesitated. He shifted his weight slightly in the chair.

''I'd better go on. But would you let me get up and walk around?''

He too wanted to go to the window, to look at the world of those who were carrying on with their normal life in the sunlight.

The previous evening he had still belonged to that world. Maigret watched him dreamily. Lapointe waited, his pencil poised.

Now, in the peaceful room on Boulevard Voltaire—a little too peaceful, almost oppressive in its calm—where the women still knitted and chatted, Doctor Pardon listened to Maigret's every word.

Nevertheless Maigret felt that he was just a link between the other man and his telephone on the shelf, between the doctor and the Polish tailor who was fighting his last battle among his five children and his hysterical wife.

A bus passed, stopped, started again after setting down two shadowy figures, and a drunk kept bumping against the walls without even faltering in his song.

—————Two—————

The Geraniums
on Rue Caulaincourt

"Good heavens!" Alice cried suddenly and stood up. "I forgot the liqueurs!"

She had changed completely. Before she was married she hardly ever came to these dinners, which must have been boring for her. In the first months of her marriage she was rarely seen, only once or twice when she was basking in her new role as a married woman, as her mother's equal, in fact.

Since she had been expecting a child she often came to Boulevard Voltaire, where she willingly acted as hostess, and she suddenly began to give more importance to the tiniest details of housewifery than even her mother did.

Her husband, a recently certified veterinary surgeon, leaped from his chair, made his wife sit down again and went into the dining room to get armagnac for the men and, for the women, a Dutch liqueur found hardly anywhere but at the Pardons'.

Like most doctors' waiting rooms, this room was badly lit, and the furniture was drab and shabby. Maigret and Pardon, facing the open window, had a l view of the glaring lights of the boulevard, where the leaves on the trees were beginning to rustle. Was there to be a change in the weather?

"Armagnac, Inspector?"

Maigret smiled vaguely at the young man, for although he realized where he was, his thoughts were still in his sunny office on that Tuesday when Josset was being interrogated.

He felt duller than he had at dinner, with the same thing weighing on his mind as on the doctor's. Pardon and he, although they had met late in life, when the working life of both was well advanced, had always been able to understand each other's half-spoken sentences. There had been a bond between them on first meeting, and they respected each other greatly.

Wasn't this because they had the same kind of honesty, not only toward others, but self-knowledge? They didn't cheat, they didn't gild the pill, they looked things squarely in the face.

And if Maigret had suddenly begun to talk that evening, it was less to distract his friend than because the phone call had reawakened in him feelings much like Pardon's.

It wasn't that he had a guilt complex. Besides, Maigret detested that expression. Nor was it a question of remorse.

Each man was obliged sometimes, through his job, the job he had chosen, to make a choice, a choice determining the fate of another. In Pardon's case it was whether a man should live or die.

There was nothing romantic in their attitude. Nor was there any dejection or rebellion, only a rather melancholy seriousness.

Young Bruart didn't quite dare to sit near them. He would have liked to know what they were talking about so quietly. But he knew that he didn't yet belong to that group, so he sat down again beside his wife.

"There were three of us in my office," Maigret was saying. "Young Lapointe, who was taking the whole thing down in shorthand, looking at me from time to time; Adrien Josset, who sometimes stood and sometimes sat on the chair; and me. I spent most of the time standing with my back to the window.

"I could see that the man was tired. He hadn't slept. He had had a lot to drink, first in the evening and then again in the middle of the night. I could see waves of lassitude sweeping over him. Sometimes he had dizzy spells, and his rather worried eyes would become fixed, expressionless, as if he were sinking into a torpor and forcing himself to snap out of it again.

"It seems cruel to have gone on in spite of that with this first interrogation, which was going to last more than three hours.

"Yet it was for his sake as much as for duty's that I kept on. On the one hand, I had no right to let slip a chance of getting a confession, if he had anything to confess. On the other, he was in such a state of nerves that he wouldn't have been able to relax without an injection or a sedative.

"He felt the need of talking, of talking right then, and if I had sent him to the cells he would have gone on talking to himself.

"There were reporters and photographers waiting

in the corridors. I could hear sudden snatches of loud conversation and laughter coming from there.

"By that time the afternoon papers had just come out and I was sure that they featured the Auteuil murder and that photographs of Josset taken that morning on Rue Lopert were blazoned over the front pages.

"It wasn't long before I had a call from Coméliau, the Magistrate, who is always anxious to get a quick solution to his cases.

" 'Is Josset there with you?'

" 'Yes.'

" 'Has he confessed?'

"The man looked at me, guessing that it was about him.

" 'I'm very busy,' I said, giving no details.

" 'Does he deny it?'

" 'I don't know.'

" 'See that he understands that it's in his own interests . . .'

" 'I'll try.'

"Coméliau isn't a bad man. He has been called my dear enemy, because we've sometimes clashed with each other.

"It's not really his fault. It stems from the idea he has of his role and therefore of his duty. In his eyes, since he is paid to defend society he must show no pity to anything that threatens to disturb the established order. I don't think he has ever known what it is to have doubts. He calmly divides the sheep from the goats and is incapable of imagining that anyone could be a mixture of the two.

"If I had told him that I hadn't yet formed an

opinion he wouldn't have believed me, or else he would have accused me of neglecting my duties.

"And yet after an hour, after two hours of questioning, I was unable to answer the silent question that Josset kept asking with pleading looks:

" 'You believe me, don't you?'

"The evening before, I hadn't met the man. I had never heard of him. If his name seemed familiar to me it was because I had taken medicines with "Josset & Virieu" on the box.

"Oddly enough, I had never set foot on Rue Lopert, which I had been rather surprised to discover that morning.

"In the little area around the parish church of Auteuil crimes are rare. And Rue Lopert, which doesn't lead anywhere, is more a private lane than a real street. It only has about twenty houses of the kind you find in any avenue in a provincial town.

"It's only a stone's throw from Rue Chardon-Lagache, and yet one feels far away from the noises of Paris. The neighboring streets, instead of being called after great men of the Republic, have authors' names: Rue Boileau, Rue Théophile-Gautier, Rue Leconte-de-Lisle.

"I wanted to go back to the house, which was different from all the others in the street. It was almost all glass and unexpected angles, built about 1925, in the Art Deco period.

"Everything was strange to me—the décor, the colors, the furniture, the layouts of the rooms, and I would have been hard put to it to say what kind of life was lived there.

"The man in front of me, fighting exhaustion and

a hangover, kept on asking with an anxious but resigned look:

" 'You believe me, don't you?'

"The Inspector at Auteuil hadn't believed him and seemed to have treated him with no consideration at all.

"At one moment I had to open the door to silence the reporters in the corridor, who were making too much noise."

For the second or third time Josset refused the sandwich he was offered. It seemed as if, knowing that his strength might fail him at any minute, he wanted to go on as far as he could, whatever the cost.

And perhaps it wasn't only because he had a Divisional Inspector facing him, a man who would have a say in his future.

He needed to convince someone, anyone, someone other than himself.

"Were you and your wife happy together?"

What would Maigret or Pardon have answered to the same question?

Josset hesitated, too.

"I think that at certain times we were very happy. . . especially when we were alone . . . especially at night. . . . We were real lovers. Do you understand? If we could have been alone more often . . ."

He wanted so much to express himself exactly.

"I don't know if you know that class of people—I didn't, either, before I was a part of it. Christine had been brought up in it. She needed it. She had many friends. She piled up social duties. Whenever she had a free minute she was on the phone. There were lunches, cocktail parties, dinners, dress rehearsals, late suppers in night clubs. There were hundreds of people we were on first-name basis with and who were always to be found at these functions.

"She loved me once, I'm sure of that. And certainly, in one sense, she still loved me."

"And you?" Maigret asked.

"I loved her, too. No one will believe it. Even our friends, who know all about us, will say it wasn't so. Yet what held us together was perhaps stronger than what is usually called love.

"We weren't lovers any more, except on rare occasions."

"How long had that been so?"

"For a few years—four or five—I don't know exactly. I couldn't even say how it came about."

"Did you quarrel?"

"Yes and no. It depends in what sense. We knew each other too well. We had no illusions left, and we couldn't cheat each other, either. We had no mercy left."

"No mercy for what?"

"For all the little faults, the tiny treacheries everyone commits. The first few times you aren't aware of them, or if you find out you are tempted to see them in such a light that they become delightful."

"You transform them into virtues?"

"Let's say that the other one grows more human, more vulnerable, because of them, so that you want to protect her, to surround her with love. You see, at the bottom of everything is the fact that I wasn't prepared for that kind of life:

"Do you know our offices on Avenue Marceau?

We have laboratories at Saint-Mandé, too, and in Switzerland and Belgium. That was, it still is, a big part of my life, the most important part. You asked me a moment ago if I was happy. There, running a business that was growing more important every day, I had a sense of accomplishment—then, suddenly, the phone would ring. Christine would ask me to meet her some place . . .''

''Did you have a feeling of inferiority toward her because of her money?''

''I don't think so. People thought—and no doubt still think—that I married her for her money.''

''Didn't you? Didn't money come into it at all?''

''No, I swear it didn't.''

''Did the business remain in your wife's name?''

''Unfortunately, no. She kept a large part, but I was given an almost equal share six years ago.''

''At your request?''

''At Christine's. You must understand that it wasn't a question, as far as she was concerned, of recognizing the results of my hard work, but of avoiding taxes without giving shares to a third party. But I can't prove that and it will count against me—as will the fact that Christine made a will in my favor. I haven't read it; I haven't seen it; I don't know where it is. She told me about it one evening when she was very depressed and thought she had cancer.''

''Was her health good?''

He hesitated, still giving the impression of a man scrupulous about details, a man who must give words their exact meaning.

''She didn't have cancer, or a bad heart, or any of those diseases you read about every week in the papers and for which people collect money in the streets. As I see it, she was nonetheless very ill. For some time she only had a few hours a day of complete lucidity, and she sometimes spent two or three days shut up in her room.''

''Didn't you sleep in the same room?''

''We did for years. Then, because I got up early and that wakened her, I moved into the room next door.''

''Did she drink a lot?''

''If you ask her friends, as you must, they will tell you that she didn't drink any more than many of them. They only saw her at her best, don't you see? They didn't know that an outing of two or three hours was preceded by several hours in bed and that the next day she had to start drinking or taking drugs as soon as she woke.''

''Don't *you* drink?''

Josset shrugged his shoulders as if to say that Maigret had only to look at him to see the answer.

''Less than she did, though. And not in such an obsessive way. If I had, the laboratories would have folded up long ago. But when I drink I act like a drunk, so those same friends will tell you that I drank more than she did. Especially since I get violent when I drink. If you haven't been in the same position, how could you understand?''

''I'm trying,'' sighed Maigret.

And then, point-blank:

''Do you have a mistress?''

''I thought we'd get to that before long! They asked me that this morning, and when I answered the detective pounced on it triumphantly, as if he'd been right on target."

"How long have you had one?"

"A year."

"In that case it started long after things grew worse between you and your wife. That began five or six years ago, didn't you say?"

"Yes, it was a long time after and had nothing to do with it. Before that I had a few affairs like anyone else, mostly short ones."

"But you've been in love for a year now?"

"It's embarrassing to use the same word I used for Christine, because it's quite different. But how else can I put it?"

"Who is she?"

"My secretary. When I said that to the detective I could tell that he had expected that answer and he was delighted with his own foreknowledge. Because it's so common it has become a joke, hasn't it? And yet . . ."

There was no more beer in the glasses. Most of the passers-by who had been walking on the bridge and on the banks of the Seine had been swallowed up again by offices and shops, where work had begun again after lunch.

"Her name is Annette Duché, she is twenty, and her father is head clerk in the Sous-Préfecture at Fontenay-le-Comte. He is in Paris just now, and I am surprised that he hasn't come here to see you since the papers came out."

"To accuse you?"

"Possibly. I don't know. Because something happens, because someone dies in dubious circumstances, everything becomes very confused from one minute to the next. Do you understand what I'm trying to say? Nothing natural, obvious, or fortuitous is left. Every action, every word takes on a damning sense. I assure you I am aware of what I am saying. I need time to organize my thoughts, but right now I want you to know that I am hiding nothing from you and that I will try as hard as I can to help you get at the truth.

"Annette had been working on Avenue Marceau for six months before I ever set eyes on her, because Monsieur Jules, the personnel officer, had put her in the shipping department, which is on another floor in the building, one I rarely go to. One afternoon my secretary was sick and I had an important report to dictate, so they sent her. We worked until 11 P.M. in the empty building, and since I felt guilty about depriving her of her dinner I took her to a local restaurant for a bite.

"That's all, really. I'm just forty and she's twenty. She reminds me of some of the girls I knew in Sète and in Montpellier. I hesitated for a long time. First I had her transferred to an office near mine, where I could keep an eye on her. I found out all about her. I was told that she was a nice girl, that when she first came to Paris she lived with an aunt on Rue Lamarck, and that after quarreling with her she had rented a small apartment on Rue Caulaincourt.

"All right, so it's silly! I even walked down Rue Caulaincourt, and I saw the pots of geraniums on her fourth-floor window sill.

"Nothing happened for almost three months. Then,

since we were setting up a branch in Brussels, I sent my secretary there and put Annette in her place.''

''Did your wife know about it?''

''I never hid anything from her. She didn't either, from me.''

''Did she have lovers?''

''If I answer that, people will say that I'm blackening her memory in order to save myself. People become sacred when they die.''

''How did she react?''

''Christine? At first she didn't react at all, just looked at me with a trace of pity in her eyes.

'' 'Poor Adrien! Have you sunk that far?'

''She kept asking me about 'the little girl,' as she called her.

'' 'Not pregnant yet? What will you do when that happens? Will you ask for a divorce?' ''

Maigret, frowning, looked at the other man with more interest.

''Is Annette pregnant?'' he asked.

''No! That at least will be easy to prove.''

''Does she still live on Rue Caulaincourt?''

''She hasn't changed her way of life at all. I didn't furnish her apartment for her; I didn't buy her a car, or jewels, or a fur coat. There are still geraniums on the window sill. There's still a walnut wardrobe with a mirror in her bedroom, and you still have to eat in the kitchen.''

His lip trembled, as if he were issuing a challenge.

''Didn't you want to change that?''

''No.''

''Did you often spend the night on Rue Caulaincourt?''

"Once or twice a week."

"Can you tell me as exactly as possible what you did yesterday and last night?"

"At what point shall I begin?"

"In the morning."

Maigret turned to Lapointe as if to tell him to take down the times very carefully.

"I got up at 7:30 as usual, and went out on the terrace for my exercise."

"That was on Rue Lopert, then?"

"Yes."

"What did you do the evening before?"

"Christine and I went to the premiere of *Témoins* at the Théâtre de la Madeleine, and then we ate at a night club on Place Pigalle."

"Did you quarrel at all?"

"No. I had a hard day ahead of me. We were thinking of changing the packaging of some of our products, and this matter of how things are presented to the public has tremendous influence on sales."

"At what time did you go to bed?"

"About 2 A.M."

"Did your wife go to bed at the same time?"

"No. I left her in Montmartre with some friends we met."

"Their name?"

"Joublin. Gaston Joublin is a lawyer. They live on Rue Washington."

"Do you know what time it was when your wife got home?"

"No. I'm a sound sleeper."

"Had you been drinking?"

"A few glasses of champagne. My head was quite clear—I was thinking only of the next day's work."

"Did you go into your wife's room in the morning?"

"I opened the door a crack amd saw she was sleeping."

"Didn't you waken her?"

"No."

"Why did you open the door?"

"To see if she had come home."

"Did she ever not come home?"

"Occasionally."

"Was she alone?"

"As far as I know, she has never brought any man back to the house."

"How many servants do you have?"

"Very few for a house the size of ours. Of course, we rarely ate at home. The cook, Madame Siran, who is really a housekeeper, doesn't live in, but lives with her son in Javel, across the Pont Mirabeau. Her son must be about thirty. He's a bachelor, his health is poor, and he works on the Métro.

"Sleeping in, there's only the housemaid—Carlotta, a Spanish girl."

"Who gets your breakfast?"

"Carlotta. Madame Siran only arrives as I'm leaving."

"Was everything the same as usual this morning?"

"Yes. . . . I'm thinking. . . . I can't think of anything special. I had a bath, dressed, went downstairs for some breakfast, and as I was getting into my car, which is parked in front of the door all night, I saw Madam Siran coming around the corner carrying her shopping basket, since she does the shopping on the way.''

''Do you have only the one car?''

''Two. I use an English two-seater, because I'm mad about sports cars. Christine has an American car.''

''Was your wife's car parked at the side of the road?''

''Yes. Rue Lopert is quiet. There's little traffic and it's easy to park there.''

''Did you go straight to Avenue Marceau?''

Josset blushed and shrugged his shoulders slightly.

''No! And naturally that will count against me too. I went to Rue Caulincourt to pick up Annette.''

''Do you go there every morning?''

''Almost. My car's a convertible. It's delightful to cross Paris early in the morning in the spring.''

''Do you and your secretary arrive at the office together?''

''For a long time I put her down at the nearest Métro station. Some employees saw us. Since everyone knew about us I preferred to be open about it, and I think I derived some pleasure from hiding nothing, from facing up to public opinion. You see, I hate that kind of smirk, those whispers, the knowing looks. Since there is nothing wrong in our relationship I don't see why . . .''

He looked for approval, but the Inspector remained impassive. It was his job.

The weather was the same as it had been the previous day, a delightful spring morning, and the little sports car coming down from Montmartre had threaded its way through the traffic, running alongside the gold-tipped railings of Parc Monceau, crossing Place des Ternes, rounding the Arc de Triomphe at a time when the crowds, still fresh at the day's start, were hurrying to their work.

"I spent the morning in discussions with my department managers, the sales manager in particular."

"In front of Annette?"

"Her desk is in my office."

It probably had tall windows looking out onto the elegant avenue with its luxury cars parked along either side.

"Did you take her to lunch?"

"No. I took an important English client who had just come over to the Berkeley."

"Did you have any word from your wife?"

"I phoned her at 2:30, when I got back to the office."

"Was she up?"

"She had just gotten up. She told me she was going to do some shopping and then have dinner with a friend, a woman."

"Did she mention her name?"

"I don't think so. I would have remembered. Since it often happened, I didn't pay much attention, and we went on with the talks we had broken off at midday."

"Did anything out of the ordinary happen during the afternoon?"

"It's not something out of the ordinary, but it has a certain importance: at about four o'clock I sent one of our errand boys to a shop in the Madeleine, to buy some hors d'oeuvres, a lobster, some Russian salad, and some fruit. I told him to buy two baskets of cherries if there were any. He put it all in my car. At six o'clock my colleagues left, as did most of the employees. At 6:15 Monsieur Jules, the oldest employee, came to see if I needed him any longer, then he left, too."

"And your partner, Monsieur Virieu?"

"He left the office at five. In spite of his years of experience, he's still an amateur and his role is largely public relations. He's the one who usually invites our foreign colleagues and our big provincial clients to lunch or dinner."

"So he should have had lunch with the Englishman?"

"Yes. He goes to the conferences, too."

"So you and your secretary were alone in the building?"

"Yes, except, of course, for the concierge. That often happens. We left the building and when we were in the car I decided to take advantage of the good weather to go and have a drink somewhere out of town. Driving relaxes me. We got to the Chevreuse valley quite quickly and had a drink in an inn."

"Didn't you and Annette ever eat in a restaurant?"

"Hardly ever. At first I avoided restaurants because I was keeping our relationship more or less secret. Then I grew fond of our little dinners on Rue Caulaincourt."

"With the geraniums at the window?"

Josset looked hurt.

"Does that seem funny to you?" he asked, a little aggressively.

"No."

"Can't you understand?"

"I think so."

"Even the lobster should gve you some clue—in my family, when I was a child, we had lobster only on special occasions. The same in Annette's family. When we had what we called our little dinners, we tried to have dishes we had wanted when we were young. In fact I did give her one present with that idea in mind—a refrigerator. It stands out a bit in the apartment, which isn't very modern. It allows us to have chilled white wine and sometimes a bottle of champagne. . . . You're not laughing at me?"

Maigret made a reassuring gesture. It was Lapointe who was smiling, as if it brought back recent memories.

"It was a little after eight when we got to Rue Caulaincourt. I must add something else. The concierge, who was motherly toward Annette before I came on the scene, turned against her after that. She used to growl obscenities at her when she passed and turned her back on me. We would go by the room where her family was seated at table, and I'd swear that the woman gave us a malicious smile when she saw us.

"It had enough effect on me to make me want to go back and ask her what was making her look so happy.

"I didn't do it, but we found out why half an hour later. Once upstairs I took my jacket off and set the table while Annette changed. I make no secret of it—that gives me pleasure, makes me feel younger. She talked to me from the next room while I looked through the half-open door at her from time to time. Her skin is fresh and clear, her body refreshing.

"I suppose this will all come out in public . . . unless I find someone who'll believe me."

His eyes closed with tiredness, and Maigret went to the wall cabinet to get him a glass of water. He didn't yet want to give him a small glass of the brandy that he always had in reserve. It was too soon. Maigret was afraid to put him into a state of nervous excitement.

"Just as we were sitting down to eat in front of the open windows Annette thought she heard something, and a moment later I, too, heard footsteps on the stairs. There was nothing strange about that, because the building has five floors and there were three flats on the floor above us.

"I wondered why she suddenly seemed embarrassed to be wearing only a blue satin peignoir. The steps halted on our landing. No one knocked at the door, but a voice said:

" 'I know you're in there! Open up!'

"It was her father. He had never come to Paris as long as I had known Annette. I'd never seen him. She had described him to me as a melancholy man, stern and withdrawn. He had been a widower for several years and lived alone, completely introverted, with nothing to take him out of himself.

" 'Just a moment, Papa!'

"She hadn't time to dress. I didn't think of putting my jacket on. She opened the door. It was me he looked at first, his eyes hard under bushy gray eyebrows.

" 'Is this the man who keeps you?' he asked his daughter.

" 'This is Monsieur Josset.'

"His look turned to the table and fell on the red splash of the lobster, on the bottle of Rhine wine.

" 'Just as they said,' he muttered as he sat down.

"He hadn't taken off his hat. He looked me over from head to foot with an unpleasant expression on his face.

" 'I suppose you keep your pajamas and slippers in the wardrobe?'

"He was right and I blushed. If he had gone into the bathroom, he would have found a razor and a shaving brush, my toothbrush and my favorite toothpaste.

"Annette, who hadn't dared to look at him at first, began to watch him and saw that he was breathing oddly, as if the climb up the stairs had had an effect on him. He was holding his body in an odd way, too.

" 'Papa, have you been drinking?' she cried.

"He never drank. He must have come to Rue Caulaincourt earlier in the day and met the concierge. Maybe she was the one who had written to tell him about the affair.

"While he waited, he must have gone into the little bar across the street, from where he must have seen us go in.

"He had drunk to give himself courage. He had a grayish complexion and his clothes hung on him as if he had once been a big man and had shrunk.

" 'So, it's true . . .'

"He peered at each of us in turn, trying to find words. Probably he was as ill at ease as we were.

"Finally he turned to me and, in a voice both threatening and ashamed, asked:

" 'What are you going to do about it?' "

———Three———

The Concierge Who
Wanted Her
Picture in the Paper

Maigret had condensed this part of the interrogation into twenty or thirty interchanges that he considered to be the most important. His narrative was not continuous. His talks with the doctor were usually sprinkled with silences during which he pulled on his pipe as if he were giving the meaning of the sentences time to take form. He knew that for his friend the words had the same meaning, evoked the same feelings as they did for him.

"A situation so common that it's only a subject for hoary old jokes. There must be tens of thousands of men in the same situation in Paris alone. Things work out all right for most of them. Drama, if there is any, is restricted to a scene between husband and wife, to separation, sometimes to divorce, and life goes on."

The man facing Maigret in the office, which smelled of spring and tobacco, was fighting a desperate battle for survival, and from time to time he looked at the Inspector to see if there was any hope left.

The scene in the apartment on Rue Caulaincourt, with its three characters, had been both dramatic and sordid. It is this particular mixture of sincerity and farce that is so difficult to make clear, difficult even to imagine after the event, and Maigret understood Josset's discouragement as he searched for his words, never satisfied with the ones he found.

"I am sure, Inspector, that Annette's father is a good man. And yet . . . He doesn't drink, I've told you that already. . . . He seems to be eating his heart out. . . . I don't know. . . . It's only a guess. . . . Perhaps it's due to remorse at not having made her happier?

"Well, yesterday, while waiting for us to get to Rue Caulaincourt, he had had a few drinks. He was in a bar, the only place he could watch the house from. He asked for a drink mechanically, or perhaps to give himself courage, and he went on without realizing it.

"When he stood in front of me he hadn't lost control of himself, but I couldn't have argued with him in his state.

"What answer could I give to his question?

"He repeated it, still giving me a hard look:

" '*What are you going to do?*'

"And I, who a few minutes earlier had nothing to blame myself for, I, who was so proud of our love that I couldn't help showing it to everyone, I suddenly felt guilty.

"We had hardly begun to eat. I can see the red of the lobster and the red of the geraniums, and Annette clutching her blue peignoir tight about her and not crying.

"I was quite moved and blurted, 'I assure you, Monsieur Duché . . .'

"He went on:

" *'You realized, I hope, that she was a virgin?'*

"I didn't find the words funny when spoken by her father. Besides, it wasn't true. Annette wasn't quite a virgin when I met her, and she hadn't tried to pretend she was.

"The funny thing is that it was indirectly because of her father that she wasn't. That solitary misanthrope admired one man only, a man of his own age who was his superior at work, whom he regarded humbly as his friend, and for whom he felt a sort of hero worship.

"Annette's first job was as a typist in this man's office, and Duché was as proud of that as some fathers are when their sons give their lives for their country.

"It's stupid, isn't it? It was with this man that Annette had her first sexual experience, which was incomplete anyway because her partner was unable to reach a climax. So because she was obsessed by the memory of the occasion, and also to prevent its happening again, she came to Paris.

"I hadn't the courage to say that to her father. I kept my mouth shut, trying to find words.

"He kept on, his voice thick:

" *'Have you told your wife?'*

"I said 'yes' without thinking, without any heed for the consequences.

" *'Does she consent to a divorce?'*

"I must admit I said 'yes' again."

Maigret gave him a hard look and asked in his turn:

"You didn't really want a divorce, did you?"

"I don't know. You want the truth, don't you? Perhaps I thought of it, but not seriously. I was happy. Let's say I had enough little pleasures to think myself a happy man, and I didn't have the courage to . . . ."

He was still forcing himself to be exact, but since he was trying to achieve an impossible degree of exactness, he grew discouraged.

"So in fact you had no reason to wish to change the status quo?"

"It's more complicated than that. With Christine, too, I had known a time . . . let's say a time when things were different. One of those times when life seems brighter. Do you understand? . . . Then reality broke through, bit by bit. I saw her change into another woman. I didn't hold it against her. I knew it had to happen. I hadn't seen the truth at the beginning, that's what it was.

"The woman that Christine became before my very eyes calls out for sympathy, too, perhaps more so than the other did. It's just that she doesn't inspire flights of rapture. It's an altogether different world."

He wiped his hand across his brow in a gesture that was becoming more and more frequent.

"I wish you could believe me! I'm trying to make you understand everything. Annette isn't the same as Christine was. I'm different, too. And I'm older now. I was happy with what she gave me, and I didn't want any more. You must find my attitude selfish, maybe even cynical. . . ."

"You didn't want to make Annette your wife and have the whole thing begin all over again. But you didn't say that to her father."

"I don't remember exactly what I said. I was ashamed, looking at him. I felt guilty. Besides, I wanted to avoid a scene. I swore I loved Annette, which is true. I promised to marry her as soon as possible."

"Did you use those exact words?"

"Perhaps. At any rate I spoke heatedly enough for Duché to be moved. I said it was a question of how long the formalities would take. To have done with the whole episode of Rue Caulaincourt, I'll tell you quickly one detail sillier than the rest. By the end I felt myself so much his son-in-law that I uncorked the champagne that we always kept in the refrigerator, and we drank each other's health.

"It was dark when I left. I got into the car and for a while I drove about the streets without knowing where I was going.

"I didn't know any longer whether I had done right or wrong. I felt I had betrayed Christine. I've never been able to kill anything. . . . And yet once, when we were staying with friends in the country, I was asked to chop off a chicken's head, and I didn't dare refuse. Everyone was watching me. It took me two attempts and I felt I was conducting an execution.

"That was a bit like what I'd just done. Because a half-drunk old man had acted the father in front of me, I had rejected fifteen years of life with Christine. I had promised, I had sworn to sacrifice her.

"I began to drink, too, in the first bar I came to. It wasn't far from Place de la République, where I was surprised to find myself when I left the bar. Then I got to the Champs-Elysées. Another bar. I had three or four drinks there, one after the other, trying to think what I should say to my wife.

"I made up sentences that I mumbled to myself to see how they sounded."

He looked at Maigret, suddenly pleading.

"I'm sorry. It's probably not the thing to do. You wouldn't have anything to drink, would you? I've kept going up to now. But it's physical, you know. When you've had too much the night before . . ."

And Maigret went over to the wall cabinet, took out the bottle of brandy, and poured a glass for Josset.

"Thank you. I'm still ashamed of myself. I have been since last night, since that grotesque scene, but not for the reasons people will think. . . .

"I didn't kill Christine. The idea never entered my head for a minute. I found many solutions to my problem, unlikely solutions, it's true, because *I* was drunk now. Even if I'd wanted to kill her, I wouldn't have had the guts."

The Pardons' telephone still hadn't rung. So the little tailor hadn't yet died and his wife was still waiting, while the children slept.

"At any moment," said Maigret, "I thought the time had come . . ."

He didn't say the time for what.

"I tried to decide, I weighed the pros and cons. My phone rang. It was Janvier, asking me to come into the detectives' office. I excused myself and went out.

"Janvier had a new edition of an afternoon paper to show me. The ink on it was still wet. A bold headline read:

DOUBLE LIFE OF ADRIEN JOSSET
VIOLENT SCENE ON RUE CAULAINCOURT

" 'Do the other papers have this too?'

" 'No, only this one.'

" 'Phone the editorial office and find out where they got it from.' "

While he waited, Maigret read the article:

We are able to give some details of the private life of Adrien Josset, whose wife was murdered last night in their house in Auteuil (see preceding article).

While friends of the couple believed them to be very close, the pharmacist had in reality been leading a double life for about a year.

He had become the lover of his secretary, Annette D—, age 20, and had set her up in an apartment on Rue Caulaincourt, where he went every morning to pick her up in his sports car and where he took her back almost every evening.

Two or three times a week Adrien Josset dined there with his mistress, and he often spent the night there.

Last night a dramatic incident took place on Rue Caulaincourt. The young lady's father, a very respectable civil servant from Fontenay-le-Comte, paying an unexpected visit to his daughter, found the couple, whose intimacy was beyond doubt, together.

The two men confronted each other in an angry exchange. We have unfortunately not been able to interview Monsieur D—, who must have left the capi-

tal this morning, but the events on Rue Caulaincourt must have some connection with the drama that later took place in the house in Auteuil.

Janvier put down the phone.

"I didn't manage to speak to the reporter, because he's not there just now."

"He must be here, waiting in the corridor with the others."

"That's possible. The girl who answered didn't want to tell me anything. She did say something about an anonymous telephone call to the editor's office at about noon, immediately after the murder was announced on the radio. I got the impression that it was the concierge who called."

Half an hour before, Josset still had a chance of putting his case to an impartial audience. He hadn't been charged. He might be a suspect, but there was no material evidence against him.

Coméliau was in his chambers, waiting for the results of Maigret's questioning, and although he wanted to have a guilty man to put before the public, he would not make a decision against the Inspector's advice.

A concierge who wanted her picture in the paper had changed the entire situation.

In the public eye Josset would now be "The Man with the Double Life," and even the thousands of men in like situations would see that there lay the motive for his wife's death.

All this was so true that Maigret heard the telephone in his office ringing already. When he went in, Lapointe, who had answered it, was saying:

"He's right here, Monsieur Coméliau. Just a moment."

Coméliau, of course!

"Have you read it, Maigret?"

"I knew all about that already," Maigret answered rather dryly.

Josset couldn't but know that it was about him and was trying to overhear.

"Did you give the information to the paper? Did the concierge tell you?"

"No. *He* did."

"Of his own free will?"

"Yes."

"Did he really meet the girl's father yesterday evening?"

"He did."

"In that case, don't you think? . . ."

"I don't know, Monsieur Coméliau. The interrogation is still going on."

"Will you be long?"

"Probably not."

"Let me know as soon as possible, and don't give the press any statement until you've seen me."

"You have my word on that."

Should he tell Josset? Wouldn't it be the right thing to do? The phone call had upset him.

"I suppose the Magistrate . . ."

"He won't do anything before he has seen me. Sit down. Try to keep calm. I still have a few questions to ask you."

"Something has happened, hasn't it?"

"Yes."

"Something that makes things worse for me?"

"In a way. I'll tell you about it in a minute. Where were you? . . . In a bar near the Etoile. . . . That will all be checked—not because we doubt your word, just routine. Do you know the name of the bar?"

"The Select. Jean, the bartender, has known me for years."

"What time was it?"

"I didn't look at my watch or at the clock in the bar, but I'd say half past nine."

"Did you speak to anyone?"

"To the bartender."

"Did you tell him your troubles?"

"No. He knew I was upset because of the way I was drinking, because I wasn't myself. He said something like:

" 'Are you feeling all right, Monsieur Josset?'

"And I said something like:

" 'Not too good.'

"Yes, that's it. I added, afraid to be taken for drunk:

" 'I've eaten something that doesn't agree with me.' "

"Were you clearheaded then?"

"I knew where I was, what I was doing, where I'd left my car. A little later I stopped at a red light. Is that what you mean by being clearheaded? . . . Still, things *were* a bit confused. The fact that I was sorry for myself, that I was getting maudlin about myself, which isn't normal for me . . ."

But he was a weak man, his story showed that clearly, and it was no less obvious in his expressions and his attitudes.

"I kept saying to myself, 'Why me?'

"I felt I'd been the victim of a plot. I even went so far as to suspect Annette of telling her father and getting him to come to Paris to make a scene that would put me in a tight spot.

"At other times I blamed Christine. Everyone will say that I owe my success to her and that it's through her I've attained a position of importance. Maybe it's true. Who knows what my career would have been like without her?

"But, on the other hand, it was she who plunged me into a world that wasn't my world, where I have never felt at ease. Only in the office did I . . ."

He shook his head.

"When I'm less tired I'll try to say it more clearly. Christine taught me a lot. There is good *and* bad in her. She isn't happy and never has been. I was going to say she never will be. You see, I can't manage to convince myself that she is dead. Doesn't that prove I didn't do it?"

Unfortunately, as other cases had shown Maigret, it didn't.

"Did you go home when you left the Select?"

"Yes."

"What were you planning to do?"

"To talk to Christine, to tell her everything, to discuss with her what I should do."

"Were you thinking about a divorce at that time?"

"It seemed the simplest solution to me, but . . ."

"But what?"

"I realized it would be difficult to get my wife to agree to it. To understand that, you'd have had to know her, and even her closest friends only knew superficial things about her. It's true that our rela-

tionship wasn't what it had been. I've already told
you we didn't sleep together any more. We quarreled
and sometimes we hated each other. But I was still
the only person who really understood her, and she
knew it. She could be herself only with me. I
never judged her. Wouldn't she have missed me? She
was so afraid of being left alone. That was why she
hated growing old, because age and loneliness were
the same in her eyes.

" 'As long as I have money, I'll be able to buy
friends, won't I?'

"She used to laugh when she said that, but it was
no joke to her.

"Was I going to tell her just like that that I was
going to leave her?"

"But you'd made up your mind?"

"Yes. . . . Not quite. . . . Not like that. . . . I
would have told her what had happened on Rue
Caulaincourt and asked her advice."

"Did you often ask her advice?"

"Yes."

"Even about business matters?"

"Important ones, yes, always."

"Do you believe that honesty was your only motive for needing to tell her all about your relationship
with Annette?"

He thought about it, truly surprised by the question.

"I see what you mean. For a start, she was older
than me. When I met her, I hardly knew Paris and
had only seen what a poor student can see here. She
taught me everything about a certain type of life, a
certain social class."

"What happened when you got back to Rue Lopert?"

"I wondered if Christine was back. It wasn't likely and I expected to have to wait awhile. That thought cheered me up a bit, since I needed to bolster up my courage."

"With another drink?"

"I suppose so. Once you've begun, you keep thinking one more glass will set you right. I saw the Cadillac parked at the door."

"Were there any lights on in the house?"

"I only noticed Carlotta's, upstairs. I let myself in with my key."

"Did you bolt the door after you?"

"I expected you'd ask that, because they asked me this morning. I suppose I did it mechanically, as a habit, but I don't remember."

"Were you still unaware of the time?"

"No. I looked at the clock in the hall. It was five past ten."

"Weren't you surprised that your wife was home so early?"

"No. She has never kept to a strict schedule, and it's hard to know exactly what she'll decide to do next."

He continued to speak of her as if she were still alive.

"Have you been to the house?" he asked.

Maigret had hardly seen it, because the men from the Public Prosecutor's Office were there, and Doctor Paul and the local Inspector, and seven or eight experts from Criminal Records.

"I must go back there," he murmured.

''You'll find a bar on the ground floor.''

The ground floor was in fact one huge room, oddly shaped, with random niches and partitions, and Maigret did indeed remember a bar almost as big as any on the Champs-Elysées.

''I poured myself a whiskey. My wife drinks nothing else. I flopped into an armchair; I needed time to draw my breath.''

''Did you put the lights on?''

''I put the hall light on when I came in, but I turned it off at once. There are no shutters on the windows. A street lamp about ten meters away lights the room well enough. Besides, it was a full moon. I remember looking at the moon for a while and even calling it to witness . . .

''I got up to pour another drink. Our glasses are very big. I sat down again in the chair, whiskey in hand, and began to think again.

''And that, Inspector, is how I fell asleep.

''The Inspector this morning didn't believe me and told me to change my story. When I refused he got angry.

''But it's true. If it happened while I was asleep I didn't hear a thing. I didn't dream, either. I don't remember anything, only a big blank . . . I can't find a better word for it.

''A pain in my side, a cramp, woke me up little by little.

''It took me some time to organize my thoughts before I stood up.''

''Did you feel drunk?''

''I don't know. Now it all seems a nightmare. I put the light on, drank a glass of water, after considering having another whiskey. Finally I started to go upstairs.''

''With the idea of waking your wife and discussing the situation with her?''

He didn't answer, but looked at the Inspector with surprise, even reproachfully. He seemed to be saying, ''Do *you* ask me that?''

And Maigret, a little embarrassed, muttered, ''Go on.''

''I went into my room, put on the light, and looked at myself in the mirror. I had a headache. My beard and the bags under my eyes looked repulsive.

''I opened Christine's door out of habit. That's when I saw her as you did this morning.''

The body half out of bed, head hanging over a fur rug spotted with blood, as were the sheets and the satin coverlet.

Doctor Paul, in a hasty examination—he was performing the autopsy while Maigret was questioning Josset—had counted twenty-one wounds inflicted by what the report, in its official language, called a sharp instrument.

So sharp in fact, and wielded with such force, that the head had almost been severed from the body.

There was silence in Maigret's office. It seemed impossible that on the other side of the windows life went on as before, that the sun was as bright, the air as soft. Two tramps were asleep under the Pont Saint-Michel, newspapers over their faces, indifferent to the noise. And two lovers sitting on the stone parapet dangled their feet above the water reflecting them.

''Try not to forget anything.''

Josset indicated that he would do his best.

"Did you put the light on in your wife's room?"

"I hadn't the courage."

"Did you go up close to her?"

"I could see enough from where I was."

"Didn't you make sure that she was dead?"

"It was obvious."

"What was your first reaction?"

"To telephone. I went to the phone and even lifted the receiver."

"To call whom?"

"I didn't know. It didn't occur to me at first to call the police. I thought first of our doctor, Doctor Badel, who is a friend."

"Why didn't you call him?"

In a whisper he repeated, "I don't know."

He put his head in his hands and thought. He fitted the part perfectly.

"It was the words, I suppose, that stopped me from phoning. What should I say?

" 'Someone has just killed Christine. Come.'

"Then I'd be asked the questions. The police would take over the house. I couldn't face them. I felt that if they pressed me, I'd collapse."

"You weren't alone in the house. The maid was upstairs."

"I know. Everything I did seems illogical, and yet you must believe that there was a certain logic in it since I acted that way and I'm not mad.

"It's also true that I had to rush to the bathroom to vomit. That wasted some time. As I leaned over the sink I thought a bit. I told myself that no one would believe me, that I'd be arrested and thrown into prison.

"And I felt exhausted. If I could only have a few hours, a few days . . . I didn't want to escape, just to have time to think. Maybe that's panic. Hasn't anyone ever told you that?"

Josset knew that many others had passed through that same office before him, people just as exhausted, just as haggard, and piece by piece had put together their string of lies or the truths that can't be communicated.

"I washed my face in cold water. I looked at myself in the mirror again. Then I rubbed my hands over my cheeks and began to shave."

"Why, *exactly*, did you shave?"

"I was thinking quickly, maybe not logically, and I was trying not to mix up the ideas rushing into my mind.

"I had decided to go away. Not by car, since I'd risk being caught too soon, and besides, I didn't have the strength for a long drive. The easiest thing would be to catch a plane, any plane, at Orly. My business requires me to travel a lot, sometimes at a moment's notice, and my passport always has some current visas.

"I calculated the time I'd need to get to Orly. I had hardly any money on me, perhaps twenty or thirty thousand francs, and there wouldn't be more than that in my wife's room, since we were in the habit of paying for everything by check. That was a complication.

"These worries stopped me thinking about what had happened to Christine. The mind fixes on small things. It was because of a little thing that I shaved. The customs officers at Orly know me. Since they know that I'm very careful about my person, perhaps too much so, they would be very surprised to see me go off on a trip unshaven.

"I had to go to the office on Rue Marceau. Although there was never much cash in the safe, I was sure I'd find several hundred thousand francs.

"I needed a suitcase, if only for appearance' sake, and I stuffed one full of underwear and toilet things. I thought of my watches. I have four, two of them valuable. That would bring me money if I needed any.

"The watches made me think of my wife's jewels. I didn't know what was going to happen. The plane might take me to the other end of Europe or to South America. I still didn't know if I would take Annette."

"Had you thought of taking her?"

"I think so, yes. Partly so as not to be alone. As my duty, too."

"Not for love?"

"I don't think so. I'm being frank. Our love was . . ."

He began again.

"Our love *is* set in a specific framework: her presence in my office, the route we take every morning from Rue Caulaincourt to Avenue Marceau, our little dinners in her apartment. I didn't *see* Annette with me in Brussels, in London, or in Buenos Aires, for example."

"But you still thought of taking her?"

"Perhaps because of my promise to her father. Then I was afraid that he might have spent the night in her apartment. What would I say to him if I found myself face to face with him in the middle of the night?''

''Did you take your wife's jewels?''

''Some of them. The ones she kept in her dressing table. The ones she had worn recently.''

''Did you do anything else?''

He hesitated, hung his head.

''No. I can't think of anything else. I put out the light. . . . I went downstairs without making a noise. . . . I hesitated about having another drink, since I felt sick to my stomach, but I had one. . . .''

''Did you take your car?''

''I decided it wasn't wise. Carlotta might have heard the engine and come down, who knows? There's a taxi stand by the church in Auteuil and I walked there.''

He picked up his empty glass and held it out to Maigret with a timid look.

''May I?''

Four

How Adrien Josset Spent the Rest of the Night

Once, talking of the notorious grillings of the French police, persistent and surprisingly effective, and the no less legendary American third degree, Maigret had said that the suspects most likely to get away with it are the simpletons. This got to the ears of a journalist, and the joke had become a stock item that the press brought out from to time in different guises.

What he had really meant to say, what he still believed, was that a simple-minded person is naturally mistrustful, always on the defensive, answers with the minimum of words without worrying about seeming truthful, and when he is later cross-examined he doesn't get upset and sticks firmly to his story.

The intelligent man, on the other hand, needs to explain himself, to dispel any doubts his questioner may have. Trying to be convincing, he anticipates questions, gives too many details, and, determined to build up a watertight case, ends up by setting his own trap.

So, when his logic is shown up, it is rare for him not to get upset and, ashamed of himself, to confess.

Adrien Josset was one of those who anticipated questions, anxious to explain facts and actions that seemed inconsistent.

Not only did he admit that they didn't fit together, but he also underlined it, sometimes seeming to be seeking the key to the mystery in speaking aloud.

Guilty or innocent, he knew enough about the mechanics of an investigation to realize that, once it had started, everything he had said and done that night would be fed through the machine sooner or later.

He said everything with so much passion that two or three times Maigret could hardly prevent a confession of the kind that came too early for his taste.

Because Maigret usually chose the time ripe for a confession. He preferred to have a wider and more personal understanding of the case first. This morning he had hardly looked at the house on Rue Lopert and he knew nothing about the people who lived there and almost nothing about the crime.

He hadn't questioned anyone else, neither the Spanish housemaid nor Madame Siran, the cook whose son had a job on the Métro and who went home to Javel every evening.

He had no idea what the neighbors were like, hadn't seen Annette Duché or the father who had been summoned rather mysteriously from Fontenay-le-Comte. And he had yet to see the head office of Josset & Virieu, Pharmaceutical Products, on Avenue Marceau, and Josset's friends, and many other more or less important people.

Doctor Paul, his autopsy finished, must have been surprised not to have the usual phone call from the

Inspector, who rarely had the patience to wait for the
written report. Up there, too, in Criminal Records,
they were working on the fingerprints found that
morning.

Torrence, Lucas, and perhaps ten or twelve detectives were carrying out the routine jobs, and, in
various offices on Quai des Orfèvres, Carlotta and
other minor witnesses were being questioned.

Maigret could have broken off the interrogation to
find out what was going on, and even Lapointe, still
hunched over his pad of notes, was surprised to see
him listening patiently, without steering the interview
in any particular direction, without trying to trap Josset.

The questions he asked were rarely technical, and
some of them seemed to have only a distant connection with the night's happenings.

"Tell me, Monsieur Josset, I suppose that at your
offices on Avenue Marceau or the laboratories of
Saint-Mandé, you sometimes have to fire people?"

"You have to do that in all businesses."

"Do you yourself do it?"

"No, I leave that to Monsieur Jules."

"Have you ever had business problems?"

"That's unavoidable, too. For example, three years
ago people said one of our products wasn't absolutely
pure and had been the cause of several deaths."

"Who dealt with that?"

"Monsieur Jules."

"I thought he was the personnel manager, not a
business manager. It seems, then . . ."

Maigret interrupted himself, then added after a bit
of thought:

"You can't bear to say unpleasant things to peo-

ple, can you? I note that when you saw Monsieur
Duché on Rue Caulaincourt you promised him anything, to get a divorce, to marry his daughter, anything rather than speak frankly.

"When you found your wife dead, you kept away
from her and didn't even put on the light. Your first
thought was to run away."

Josset hung his head.

"It's true. I panicked—there's no other word for
it."

"You got a taxi near the church in Auteuil?"

"Yes. A gray 403. The driver was from the Midi,
by his accent."

"You asked to be taken to Avenue Marceau?"

"Yes."

"What time was it?"

"I don't know."

"You must have passed several lighted clocks.
You meant to take a plane. You often travel by
plane. Therefore you know the timetables of several
airlines. It was very important for you to know the
time."

"I know all that but I can't explain it. Things
don't always happen the way you expect them to
when you are thinking about them with a cool head."

"Did you have the taxi wait when you got to
Avenue Marceau?"

"I didn't want to attract attention. I paid the man
and walked across the sidewalk. For a moment, as I
went through my pockets, I thought I had forgotten
my key."

"Did that worry you?"

"No. I meant to leave Paris, but I was fatalistic

about it. Besides, I found the key in a pocket I don't normally put it in. I went in.''

''Wasn't there a risk of waking up the concierge?''

''If I had done so, I would have said that I needed some papers for a last-minute business trip. It didn't worry me.''

''Did he hear you?''

''No. I went up to my office. I opened the safe, took the four hundred and fifty thousand francs in it, amd wondered where to hide them in case I was searched at customs. I didn't worry too much about it, since I never have been searched. I sat in my chair, not moving, for about ten minutes, looking around me.''

''Was that when you decided not to leave?''

''I felt too tired. I had no strength left.''

''Strength for what?''

''For going to Orly, for buying a ticket, waiting, showing my passport, being afraid . . .''

''Afraid of being arrested?''

''Of being questioned. I kept thinking of Carlotta. She might have come downstairs. Even when I landed at a foreign airport, there was still the risk of being questioned. At best, I would have had to start a new life alone.''

''Did you put the money back in the safe?''

''Yes.''

''What did you do then?''

''The suitcase was hampering me. I wanted a drink. It became an obsession. I was sure that even though it hadn't helped before, a little alcohol would restore my self-control. I had to walk to the Etoile to get another taxi. I said:

" 'First of all, stop at a bar.'

"The taxi had only to go about two hundred meters. I left the suitcase in it and I went into a strip-tease place without noticing which one it was. I refused to follow the maître d'hôtel to a table. I leaned on the bar and ordered a whiskey. A hostess asked me to buy her a drink, and I did, to avoid a scene.

"On the dance floor another woman was taking off black underclothes and uncovering more and more white skin.

"I had two drinks. I paid. I went out and got into my taxi again.

" 'Which station do you want?' the driver asked.

" 'I want to go to Auteuil. Go by Rue Chardon Lagache. I'll tell you when to stop.'

"My suitcase was making me feel guilty. I stopped the taxi about a hundred and fifty meters from my house and before I went in I reassured myself that there were no lights on in the house. I only lit the lights I had to, and I put my wife's jewels back and put away my clothes and toilet articles. I expect they'll find my fingerprints on the dressing table and on the jewels if they haven't done so already."

"So you went into her bedroom again?"

"I had to."

"Didn't you look?"

"No."

"And you still didn't think of phoning the police?"

"I kept putting it off."

"What did you do then?"

"I went out and wandered around the streets."

"Which way did you go?"

Josset hesitated, and Maigret, watching him, frowned and pressed the point rather impatiently.

"It's an area you're familiar with. You've lived there for fifteen years. Even if you were preoccupied or upset you must have recognized some places you passed."

"I do remember the Pont Mirabeau, where I somehow found myself. I couldn't think how I'd got there."

"Did you cross it?"

"Not all the way. I leaned on the parapet somewhere near the middle of the bridge and watched the Seine go by."

"What were you thinking about?"

"That I was going to be arrested and that for weeks, if not months, I would be struggling with exhausting and painful problems."

"Did you go home again?"

"Yes. I would have liked another drink before going to the police, but everything was closed. I had to take a taxi again."

"Does Annette Duché have a telephone?"

"I had one put in for her."

"Did you never think of calling her to tell her what had happened?"

He thought.

"Perhaps. I don't remember. Anyway, I didn't."

"Did you wonder at all who could have killed your wife?"

"I was more concerned with the fact that I would be the one who would be accused."

"According to the report I have here you appeared at 3:30 at the Auteuil Police Station on the corner of

Boulevard Exelmans and Rue Chardon-Lagache. You gave your card to the policeman on duty and asked to see the Inspector in person. He told you that wasn't possible at that hour of the night and took you to Detective Jeannet's office.''

''He didn't tell me his name.''

''First the detective questioned you briefly, and when you had given him your key he sent a car to Rue Lopert. I have here the more detailed statements you made later. I haven't read them. Are they correct?''

''I think so. It was very hot in that office. I suddenly felt exhausted and wanted to sleep. The detective's manner of asking questions, sometimes brutal, sometimes ironical, annoyed me.''

''You seem to have been able to sleep for two hours.''

''I don't know how long it was.''

''Do you have anything to add?''

''I don't think so. Perhaps some things will come back later. I'm exhausted. It seems as if everything is against me, that I'll never be able to prove the truth. I didn't kill Christine. I have always tried never to hurt anyone. Do you believe me?''

''I haven't any opinion. Will you type out your notes, Lapointe?''

And to Josset:

''You've had enough for just now. When they bring you the typed statement, read it and sign it.''

He went into the neighboring office and sent Janvier to keep Josset company.

The performance had taken three hours.

*　　*　　*

While he was silently watching the lights on Boulevard Voltaire, Maigret heard his wife cough slightly. He turned toward her and saw her make a little sign to him.

She was reminding him of the time. It was later than they usually stayed. Alice was saying good night to her mother, because she and her husband had to go home to Maisons-Alfort. Pardon kissed his daughter on the forehead.

"Good night!"

Just as the young people reached the door, the phone rang loudly—more loudly, it seemed, than usual. Madame Pardon looked at her husband, and he went slowly to answer it.

"Doctor Pardon."

It was Madame Kruger. Her voice was less shrill, less vibrant than it had been a short while before. Now those standing at a distance could barely hear a murmur from the receiver.

"No, no," Pardon was saying gently. "You can't blame yourself at all. . . . It's not your fault, I assure you. . . . Are the children up? . . . Haven't you got a neighbor you can take them to? . . . Listen, I'll be with you in half an hour at the latest. . . ."

He listened a little longer, murmuring something from time to time.

"Yes . . . yes, of course. . . . You've done all you could. . . . I'll take care of that. . . . Yes . . . yes . . . I'll see you in a few minutes."

He hung up and sighed. Maigret was standing up. Madame Maigret had wrapped up her knitting and put on her spring coat.

"Is he dead?"

"He died a few minutes ago. I must go over there. She's going to need help."

They went downstairs together. The doctor's car was parked at the curb.

"Don't you want a lift?"

"No, thank you. We'd prefer to walk a little."

That was part of the tradition. Madame Maigret took her husband's arm automatically, and they walked home slowly in the calm evening air along the empty sidewalks.

"Were you telling him about the Josset case?"

"Yes."

"Were you able to get to the end?"

"No. I'll tell him the rest some other time."

"You did all you could."

"Like Pardon this evening. Like the tailor's wife."

She gripped his arm more tightly.

"It's not your fault."

"I know."

There were some cases like that which he didn't like to remember, and, paradoxically, they were the ones he had taken most to heart.

For Pardon, the Jewish tailor on Rue Popincourt had previously been almost unknown, one sick person among many. Now, because of a high-pitched voice on the telephone, because of a decision taken at the end of a family dinner, because of some words spoken wearily, Maigret was sure that his friend would always remember him.

Josset, too, had had an important place in Maigret's thoughts for a time.

While Lapointe was typing his shorthand notes, while telephones shrilled in all the offices, while the journalists and the photographers grew more impatient, Maigret wandered here and there on the premises of the Police Headquarters, grave, preoccupied, his shoulders hunched.

As he had expected, he found the Spanish maid being questioned by Torrence in a distant office. She was a woman of about thirty, quite pretty, with a cheeky look, but her lips were thin and hard.

Maigret looked her over from head to foot, then turned to Torrence.

"What does she say?"

"She says she knows nothing. She was sleeping and was awakened by the Auteuil police, who were making a racket on the first floor."

"At what time did her mistress come home?"

"She doesn't know."

"Wasn't she in the house?"

"I had permission to go out," the young woman interrupted.

She hadn't been asked, but she was annoyed to see how little notice was being taken of her.

"She had to meet her boyfriend by the Seine."

"At what time?"

"Half past eight."

"When did she get back?"

"At ten."

"Didn't she see any lights on in the house?"

"She says she didn't."

"I don't just say so! I didn't!"

She still had a strong accent.

"Did you go through the big room on the ground floor?" Maigret asked her.

"No. I went in the back door."

"Were there any cars in front of the house?"

"I saw Madame's was there."

"And Monsieur's?"

"I didn't notice."

"Don't you usually make sure that they don't need anything when you come in?"

"No. What they did in the evenings was their own affair, not mine."

"Didn't you hear any noises?"

"I would have said so if I had."

"Did you go straight to sleep?"

"As soon as I had washed."

Maigret growled to Torrence:

"Get hold of her boyfriend and check."

Carlotta's spiteful look followed him to the door.

Back in the detectives' office, he picked up a phone.

"Get me Doctor Paul, please. He may still be at the Forensic Institute. If not, call his house."

He had to wait for a few minutes.

"This is Maigret. Do you have any news?"

He took notes out of habit. He didn't have to, since he would get the full report a little later.

The throat wound had been one of the first and was enough to cause death within a minute at most. The killer had therefore kept on stabbing viciously at a body already drained of most of its blood.

The alcohol level of the blood showed, according to the forensic surgeon, that Christine Josset was drunk when she was killed.

She had not eaten. No food was being digested in the stomach. Her liver was, in fact, in a very bad state.

As to the time of death, Doctor Paul placed it tentatively between 10 P.M. and 1 A.M.

"Can't you be more precise?"

"Not just now. One more detail that may interest you. The woman had had sexual intercourse a few hours before death, at the earliest."

"Could it have been half an hour before?"

"It's possible."

"Ten minutes?"

"Scientifically, I can't answer that."

"Thank you, Doctor."

"What does he say?"

"Who?"

"The husband."

"That he's innocent."

"Do you believe him?"

"I don't know."

Another phone rang. A detective signaled to Maigret that it was for him.

"Is that you, Inspector? This is Coméliau. Have you finished your interrogation?"

"A few minutes ago."

"I'd like to see you."

"I'll be right over."

He was just leaving the room when Bonfils came in, excited.

"I was just going to knock on your door, Chief. . . . I've just come from the house. . . . I spent two hours with Madame Siran, questioning her and making another careful inspection of the house. I've got something new."

"What?"

"Has Josset confessed?"

"No."

"Hasn't he told you about the dagger?"

"What dagger?"

"Madame Siran and I were examining Josset's room when I saw she was looking for something and seemed rather surprised. It was difficult for me to get her to speak, because I think she likes the master better than the mistress, for whom she didn't have a very high regard. Finally she muttered:

" 'The German dagger.'

"It seems it's one of those Commando knives that some people keep as a war souvenir."

Maigret looked surprised.

"Was Josset in the Commandos during the war?"

"No, he wasn't in the war at all. He received an exemption because of his health. It was someone in his office, a Monsieur Jules, who brought it back and gave it to him."

"What did Josset do with it?"

"Nothing. It sat on a small desk in his bedroom and he probably used it as a letter opener. It has disappeared."

"Has it been gone long?"

"Since this morning. Madame Siran is quite sure about that. She takes care of her employer's room, while the Spanish girl sees to Madame Josset's room and clothes."

"Did you look everywhere?"

"I searched the house from top to bottom, including the attic and the cellar."

Maigret almost went back to his office to ask Josset about it. He didn't do so because the Magistrate was waiting for him, and Coméliau was hard to please. Then again, he needed time to think.

He passed through the glass door separating Police Headquarters from the Palais de Justice and went along several corridors before knocking at the familiar door.

"Sit down, Maigret."

The afternoon newspapers were spread out on the desk, showing their banner headlines and their photographs.

"Have you read those?"

"Yes."

"Does he still deny it?"

"Yes."

"But he admits that the scene on Rue Caulaincourt did take place yesterday evening, a few hours before his wife's death?"

"He told me about it of his own accord."

"I suppose he says it's a coincidence?"

As usual, Coméliau, mustache trembling, was beginning to lose his temper.

"At eight o'clock in the evening the father finds him with his young daughter, Josset's mistress. The two men face each other, and the father demands redress."

Maigret sighed wearily:

"Josset promised he would divorce his wife."

"And marry the daughter?"

"Yes."

"But to do that, Josset would have had to give up his wealth and his position."

"That's not quite true. For some years Josset has owned one third of the drug company."

"Do you think his wife would have agreed to the divorce?"

"I don't think anything, sir."

"Where is he?"

"In my office. One of my detectives is typing out the record of the interrogation. Josset will read it and sign."

"And then? What are you going to do with him then?"

Coméliau felt Maigret's reluctance to speak, and that angered him.

"I expect you're going to ask me to let him go free, to tell me that you wish to have him watched by your detectives in the hope that he'll betray himself in some way or other."

"No."

That cut the Magistrate short.

"Do you think he's guilty?"

"I don't know."

"Listen, Maigret. If ever a case was clear-cut, it's this one. Four or five of my friends who knew Josset and his wife well have been on the phone to me . . ."

"Are they against him?"

"They've always known what he is."

"And what is that?"

"An ambitious and unscrupulous man who took advantage of Christine's passion. But when she began to grow old, he found he needed a younger mistress and didn't hesitate to take one."

"I'll send you the statement when it's ready."

"And until then?"

"I'm keeping Josset in my office. You'll decide what to do with him."

"No one would stand for my setting him free."

"That's quite likely."

"No one, you understand, no one, will believe he is innocent. I will read your report before I sign his committal, but you may take it that my mind is already made up."

He didn't like the look on the Inspector's face. He called him back.

"Do you have anything to say in his favor?"

Maigret didn't answer. He hadn't anything to say. Except that Josset told him that he hadn't killed his wife.

Perhaps that was too easy, too obvious.

He went back to his office, where Janvier showed him the man asleep in his chair.

"You can go. Tell Lapointe I'm back."

Maigret sat down, fiddled around with his pipes, and chose one—which he was lighting when Josset opened his eyes and looked at him without saying anything.

"Do you want to go on sleeping?"

"No. I'm sorry. Have you been here long?"

"A few minutes."

"Have you seen the Magistrate?"

"I've just come from his office."

"Am I going to be arrested?"

"I think so."

"It was inevitable, wasn't it?"

"Do you know a good lawyer?"

"Several of my friends are good lawyers. I wonder if I wouldn't rather have a complete stranger."

"Tell me, Josset . . ."

The man shuddered, sensing that something unpleasant was coming after those simple words.

"Yes?"

"Where did you hide the knife?"

There was a slight pause.

"I did wrong. I should have told you about it."

"You went to throw it in the Seine from the Pont Mirabeau, didn't you?"

"Has it been found?"

"Not yet. Tomorrow morning divers will go down for it and they'll find it."

The man was silent.

"Did you kill Christine?"

"No."

"Yet you took the trouble to go all the way to the Pont Mirabeau to throw your knife into the Seine."

"No one will believe me, not even you."

The "not even you" was a compliment to Maigret.

"Tell me the truth."

"It was when I went home and put my suitcase away. I saw the dagger in my room . . ."

"Were there any bloodstains on it?"

"No. At that time I was thinking of what I was going to say to the police. I already realized that my story would seem hard to believe. Although I hadn't looked carefully at the body, what I had seen made a knife seem the likely weapon.

"When I saw mine lying out on my desk, I told myself that the police would make the connection at once."

"But there wasn't any blood on it!"

"If I had killed her, and if there had been any,

wouldn't I have been careful to clean the weapon? I hadn't thought carefully enough when I fastened my suitcase with the intention of taking a plane. The presence of the knife a few feet away from the body overwhelmed me, and I removed it. It was Carlotta who told you, wasn't it? She has never been able to stand me.''

''It was Madame Siran.''

''I'm a little surprised at that. But I should have expected it. From now on I suppose I can't count on anyone any more.''

Lapointe came into the office holding some type-written pages, which he placed in front of his superior. Maigret handed one copy to Josset and scanned the other himself.

''Get hold of a diver for tomorrow morning. At dawn by the Pont Mirabeau.''

One hour later the photographers were finally able to take pictures of Adrien Josset leaving Maigret's office with handcuffs on.

It was precisely because of the reporters and photographers that Coméliau had insisted on handcuffs.

Five

The Obstinate Silence of Doctor Liorant

Certain details of the case were etched more sharply than others on Maigret's memory, and several years later he could remember the taste and smell of the sudden shower on Rue Caulaincourt as clearly as any childhood recollection.

It was 6:30 in the evening and when it began to rain the sun, already turning red above the rooftops, was not obscured: the sky continued to glow and some windows still reflected the light, while a solitary pearly-gray cloud with silver edges, slightly darker at the center, floated like a balloon over the area.

It didn't rain everywhere in Paris, and in the evening Madame Maigret assured her husband that none had fallen on Boulevard Richard-Lenoir.

The raindrops seemed wetter, more transparent than usual, and at first they left big black rings on the dusty road as they landed one by one.

As he raised his head, the Inspector saw four pots of geraniums on the sill of an open window, and then he was hit in the eye by a raindrop so large that it almost hurt.

The open window made him think that Annette was already home, and he went into the building, passing the concierge's room, and looked in vain for an elevator. He was about to start climbing the stairs when a door opened behind him. An unpleasant voice called:

"Where do you think you're going?"

He found himself face to face with the concierge, who wasn't at all like the idea he had formed from Josset's tale. He had imagined her as middle-aged and careless about her appearance. But she was an attractive woman of about thirty, with a good figure. Only her voice grated, vulgar and aggressive.

"To see Mademoiselle Duché," he answered politely.

"She isn't back yet."

Later he was to remember that it was at this precise moment that he wondered why some people seem disagreeable at once, for no particular reason.

"It must be about time for her to come in, isn't it?"

"She comes and goes as she likes."

"Was it you who phoned the newspaper?"

She stood in her doorway and did not invite him in.

"What of it?" she asked defiantly.

"I'm a policeman."

"I know. I recognized you. You don't impress me."

"When Monsieur Duché came to see his daughter yesterday, did he tell you his name?"

"He even stayed a quarter of an hour in my room, chatting."

"So he came before, when his daughter wasn't in. In the afternoon, I suppose?"

"About five o'clock."

"Was it you who wrote to Fontenay?"

"If I had I would only have been doing my duty, and it wouldn't be any concern of anybody's. But it wasn't me. It was the young lady's aunt."

"Do you know her aunt?"

"We shop in the same stores."

"Did you tell her what was going on?"

"She guessed all by herself."

"Did she tell you she was going to write?"

"We talked about it."

"When Monsieur Duché came, did you tell him about Monsieur Josset?"

"I answered his questions and advised him to come back a little later, after seven."

"When the girl came in, didn't you warn her?"

"I'm not paid to do that."

"Was Monsieur Duché very angry?"

"He could hardly believe it, poor man."

"Did you go up a little later to find out what was going on?"

"I took a letter up to the fourth floor."

"Did you stop on the third-floor landing?"

"I might have done, to catch my breath. What are you trying to make me say?"

"You spoke of a violent scene."

"To whom?"

"To the reporter."

"The papers print what they choose to. Look! There she is, *your* young lady."

It wasn't one girl but two who came into the

building and went toward the stairs without even looking at the concierge or Maigret. The first was blond and very young. She wore a navy-blue suit and a light-colored hat. The second, thinner, harder, must have been about thirty-five and walked like a man.

"I thought you came to talk to her."

Maigret controlled his anger, for this uncalled-for spitefulness hit him like a physical blow in the stomach.

"I'll talk to her, don't worry. It's quite likely I'll have another word with you, too."

He could have kicked himself for this rather childish threat. He waited to go upstairs until he had heard a door open and close again above.

He stopped for a moment on the third floor to get his breath back, and knocked at the door a minute later. He heard whispering, then footsteps. It was not Annette but her friend who opened the door a crack.

"What do you want?"

"Inspector Maigret from Police Headquarters."

"Annette, it's the police!"

She must have been in her bedroom, perhaps changing her suit, which must have gotten wet in the rain.

"I'm coming."

Everything was disappointing. The geraniums were certainly in place, but they were the only things that corresponded to the Inspector's mental picture. The apartment was commonplace, without a single personal touch. The famous dining-room-cum-kitchen where the little dinners had been held had dull gray walls, and the furniture was just like that in any other cheap room.

Annette hadn't changed, only run a comb through her hair. She, too, was a disappointment. True, she had a kind of freshness, the kind of freshness one has at twenty, but she was ordinary, with large, prominent blue eyes. She reminded Maigret of the photographs found in provincial photographers' windows, and he would have bet that at forty she would be very fat, with a hard mouth.

"I'm sorry, mademoiselle . . ."

The friend went reluctantly toward the door.

"I'll leave you."

"Why? You're not in the way."

And, to Maigret:

"This is Jeanine, who works with me on Avenue Marceau. She was kind enough to come home with me. Sit down, Inspector."

He would have found it difficult to say what he felt was wrong. He felt annoyed with Josset for having idealized this girl, who, although her eyes were a little red, hardly seemed upset at all.

"Has he been arrested?" she asked, mechanically tidying up a few things nearby.

"The magistrate signed a committal order this afternoon."

And Jeanine advised her:

"You'd better let the Inspector speak."

It wasn't an official questioning, and Coméliau would have been furious had he known that Maigret had taken this step on his own initiative.

"What time was it when you heard about the murder?"

"Just when we were leaving the office for lunch. One of the clerks has a transistor radio. He told the others what had happened, and Jeanine told me."

"Did you have lunch as usual?"

"What else could I do?"

"She wasn't hungry, Inspector. I had to take her upstairs again. She kept bursting into tears."

"Is your father still in Paris?"

"He left at nine this morning. He wanted to be back in Fontenay today because he only took two days' leave and he starts work again tomorrow."

"Did he stay in a hotel?"

"Yes. Near the station. I don't know which one."

"Did he stay here long yesterday evening?"

"About an hour. He was tired."

"Did Josset promise him he would get a divorce and marry you?"

She blushed and looked at her friend as if asking advice.

"Did Adrien tell you that?"

"Did he?"

"It was mentioned."

"Was there a formal promise?"

"I think so."

"Before that, did you hope he would marry you one day?"

"I didn't think of it."

"Didn't he ever speak of the future?"

"No, not really."

"Were you happy?"

"He was kind to me, very attentive."

Maigret didn't dare to ask her if she loved him, because he feared she would lie again, and Annette asked:

"Do you think he'll be convicted?"

"Do you think he killed his wife?"

She blushed and again looked to her friend for advice.

"I don't know. The radio says he did, and the newspapers . . ."

"You know him well. Do you think he had it in him to kill his wife?"

Instead of answering directly, she muttered:

"Do you suspect anyone else?"

"Was your father hard on him?"

"Papa was sad, completely crushed. He never thought such a thing could happen to his daughter. He still thinks I'm a little girl."

"Did he threaten Josset?"

"No. He wouldn't threaten anyone. He just asked him what he was planning to do and suddenly, of his own accord, Adrien started talking about divorce."

"Wasn't there any quarrel, any shouting?"

"Certainly not. I don't know how it came about, but we ended up drinking champagne. My father seemed relieved. There was even a glint in his eyes that I've hardly ever seen before."

"And after Adrien left?"

"We talked about the wedding. My father was sorry that it couldn't be a white wedding, in Fontenay, because people would snigger."

"Did he have any more to drink?"

"He emptied the bottle that we hadn't finished before Adrien left."

Her friend gave her a look warning her not to say too much.

"Did you take him back to his hotel?"

"I offered, but he didn't want me to."

"Didn't your father seem upset to you, different from usual?"

"No."

"He's not a drinking man, I believe. Have you ever seen him have a drink in Fontenay?"

"Never. Only a little wine with water, at mealtimes. When he had to meet someone in a café, he ordered mineral water."

"But he had been drinking yesterday before he made his unexpected visit."

"Don't answer without thinking," advised Jeanine with a knowing look.

"What should I say?"

"The truth," answered Maigret.

"I think he'd had a glass or two while he was waiting."

"Didn't you notice his speech was awkward?"

"His speech was a bit slurred, I noticed that. Still, he knew what he was saying and what he was doing."

"Didn't you call his hotel to make sure he'd returned safely?"

"No. Why?"

"Didn't he call you this morning to say good-bye?"

"No. We never phone each other. We've never gotten into the habit. At home in Fontenay we don't have a telephone."

Maigret preferred not to pursue the matter.

"Thank you, mademoiselle."

"What does he say?" she asked, worried again.

"Josset?"

"Yes."

"He says he didn't kill his wife."

"Do you believe him?"

"I don't know."

"How is he? Does he need anything? He isn't too depressed?"

Each word was badly chosen, not strong enough in proportion to what had happened.

"He's quite depressed. He spoke a lot about you."

"Didn't he ask to see me?"

"That's not up to me now, but to the Magistrate."

"Didn't he give you any message?"

"He didn't know I was coming to see you."

"I expect I'll be called as a witness?"

"Very likely. That depends on the Magistrate, too."

"May I keep on going to the office?"

"I don't see why not."

He felt he had better leave. As he went through the main door, Maigret glimpsed the concierge. She was eating, sitting opposite a man in shirt sleeves. She threw him a mocking look.

It was perhaps the Inspector's state of mind that made him find everything and everyone disappointing. He crossed the street and went into a little local bar where four men were playing cards, while two others, elbows on the counter, were talking to the proprietor.

He didn't know what to drink, asked for the first drink he saw the label of, and remained silent for quite a long time, scowling, in about the same place Annette's father must have stood the previous evening.

If he turned his head, he could see the entire front of the building across the street, with four pots of geraniums at one of the windows. Jeanine, hiding in the shadows, had seen him cross the street and was talking to her invisible friend.

"You had a customer who spent a long time here yesterday, didn't you?"

The proprietor picked up a newspaper and tapped the article about the Josset case.

"You mean the father?"

And, turning to the others:

"It's funny. I knew right away something was up. In the first place he wasn't the kind of man to lean at the bar for over an hour. He asked for some mineral water, and I had already picked up the bottle when he changed his mind.

" 'No, give me . . .'

"He looked at the bottles and seemed unable to make up his mind.

" 'Liquor . . . any kind . . .'

"It's not common for someone to ask for liquor before dinner.

" 'A brandy? A calvados?'

" 'A calvados, please.'

"It made him cough. It was easy to see he wasn't used to it. He kept on looking at the door across the street, then at the Metro exit, a little farther away. Two or three times I saw his lips move as if he were talking to himself."

The proprietor interrupted himself, frowning.

"Aren't you Inspector Maigret?"

And since Maigret didn't deny it:

"Hey, everybody, it's the famous Inspector Maigret. So that pharmacist has confessed, has he? I've had my eye on him, too, for a long time. Because of his car. You don't get many sports cars around here.

"It was mostly in the mornings I used to see him, when he came to get the girl. He parked right in front of the door and looked up. The young lady would wave at the window, and she'd come out to join him a minute or two later."

"How many glasses of calvados did your customer have?"

"Four. Each time he asked for another he looked ashamed, as if he was afraid I would take him for an alcoholic."

"Did he come back later?"

"I didn't see him again. This morning I saw the girl. She waited a while on the sidewalk, then went to the Métro."

Maigret paid and went toward Place Clichy, looking for a taxi as he went. He found a free one just as he was passing the Montmartre cemetery.

"Boulevard Richard-Lenoir, please."

Nothing else happened that evening. He dined alone with his wife, to whom he said nothing at all, while she, knowing his moods, took care not to ask him any questions.

The investigation went on as usual in other ways. The machinery of the police force had been set in motion, and the Inspector would find several reports on his desk the next day.

For this case, for no particular reason and against his usual practice, he decided to make a sort of private dossier.

The times, in particular, seemed to have a great importance, and he racked his brains to reconstruct the sequence of events, hour by hour.

Since the crime had been discovered in the morning, or rather toward the end of the night, the morning papers couldn't have anything on it, and it was the radio that first made public the drama of Rue Lopert.

At the time of this broadcast the reporters were camped in front of Josset's house in Auteuil, where the men from the Public Prosecutor's Office had descended in force. .

Between noon and one o'clock the first afternoon papers spoke briefly of the event.

One daily only, contacted by the concierge of the building on Rue Caulaincourt, brought out the story of Duché's visit to his daughter and his meeting with Annette's lover, in its third edition.

All this time the head clerk's train was traveling to Fontenay-le-Comte, and the fresh news couldn't reach him.

Later on they found at least one of his traveling companions, a grain merchant from near Niort. The two men were strangers to each other. When the train left Paris the compartment was full, but after Poitiers only the two of them remained.

"I thought I knew him by sight though I couldn't remember where I had met him. I nodded to him politely. He looked startled, a bit annoyed, and huddled into his corner.

"He seemed a bit under the weather. His eyelids were red, as if he hadn't slept. When the train stopped at Poitiers, he went to the buffet for a bottle of Vichy water, which he gulped down."

"Was he reading?"

"No. He watched the countryside going by, in a vague sort of way. From time to time he closed his

eyes, and finally he went to sleep. When I got home
I suddenly remembered where I'd seen him—at the
Sous-Préfecture at Fontenay, where I sometimes have
to go to sign papers.''

Maigret, who had made the trip especially to see
the grain merchant—his name was Lousteau—tried
to find out more. He seemed to be looking for something he couldn't explain.

''Did you notice his clothes?''

''I couldn't say what color they were—they were
dark, not very well cut.''

''Weren't they crumpled, as if he had spent the
night out of doors?''

''I didn't notice. I was looking at his face. Wait!
There was a raincoat in the luggage rack, on top of
his suitcase.''

It took some time to find the hotel where Annette's
father had stayed, the Hôtel de la Reine et de Poitiers, near the Gare d'Austerlitz.

It was a cheap hotel, dimly lit and gloomy, but
clean, mainly patronized by regulars. Martin Duché
had stayed there several times. His previous visit had
been two years before, when he had brought his
daughter to Paris.

''He had room 53. He didn't take any meals in the
hotel. He arrived Tuesday on the 3:53 P.M. train and
went out almost immediately after filling in his form,
saying he would only be staying one night.''

''What time did he come in in the evening?''

There they ran into difficulties. The night porter,
who had a cot in the office, was a Czech who hardly
spoke any French and who had twice been a patient
in Sainte-Anne, the mental hospital. The name Duché

didn't mean anything to him, nor did a description. When asked about room 53, he looked at the keyboard, scratching his head.

"He comes . . . he goes . . . he comes back . . . he leaves," he muttered angrily.

"When did you go to bed?"

"Not before midnight. I always shut the door and go to bed at midnight. That's orders."

"Don't you know if number 53 was back?"

The poor man did what he could but he couldn't do much. He hadn't been working at the hotel two years before, when Duché last stayed there.

He was shown a photograph.

"Who is it?" he asked, anxious to please his questioners.

Maigret, stubborn as usual, had gone so far as to look for the two people who had had rooms on either side of number 53. One of them lived in Marseilles and could be reached by telephone.

"I don't know a thing. I came in at eleven and I didn't hear a thing."

"Were you alone?"

"Of course."

He was a married man. He had come to Paris without his wife. And they were sure that he at least had not spent the night alone.

As for number 51, a Belgian who was only traveling through France, it proved impossible to trace him.

At a quarter to eight in the morning, at any rate, Duché had been in his room and had ordered breakfast. The maid hadn't noticed anything odd except that he asked for three cups of coffee.

"He seemed tired."

That was vague. It was impossible to get her to say any more. At half past eight, without having taken a bath, Duché had gone downstairs and paid his bill to the cashier, who knew him.

"He was the same as usual. I've never seen him look happy. He looked like a sick man. He stood still as if to listen to his heart beating. I knew someone else like that, a good customer, a man who came once a month. He had the same look, the same gestures, and one morning he fell dead on the stairs without even having time to call for help."

Duché had caught his train. That's where he was, sitting opposite the grain merchant, when Maigret was interrogating Josset on Quai des Orfèvres.

At that same time a reporter on a morning paper, after rushing to Rue Caulaincourt, called his correspondent in Fontenay-le-Comte.

The concierge hadn't told Maigret about the visit of this journalist, to whom she had given Annette's father's name and address.

These tiny facts were all jumbled together, and it took time and patience to turn them into a more or less logical picture.

When the train stopped at Fontenay-le-Comte that afternoon, Martin Duché still didn't know anything about it. Nor did the people of Fontenay, for the radio had not yet given the name of their fellow citizen, and only by guessing could they have made a connection between the head clerk and the Sous-Préfecture and the drama on Rue Lopert.

Only the newspaper correspondent knew what was going on. He had gotten hold of a photographer. They were both waiting on the platform, and when

Duché stepped out of the train he was surprised to be welcomed by a flash gun.

"May I, Monsieur Duché?"

He blinked, bewildered and confused.

"I suppose you haven't yet heard the news?"

The reporter was polite. The head clerk seemed like a man who doesn't understand what is happening to him. Suitcase in hand, raincoat over his arm, he went toward the exit, handing his ticket to the ticket collector, who greeted him by touching his hand to his cap. The photographer took another picture. The reporter drew closer to Annette's father.

They went down Rue de la République together in the sunshine.

"Madame Josset was murdered last night."

The newspaperman, Pecqueur by name, had a baby face, plump cheeks, and the same protuberant eyes as Annette. He had red hair, his whole appearance was casual, and, in order to make himself look important, he was smoking a pipe that was much too big for him.

Maigret interviewed him, too, in the back room of the Café de la Poste, by the empty billiard table.

"What was his reaction?"

"He stopped in his tracks and stared at me as if he suspected me of setting a trap for him."

"A trap? Why?"

"No one in Fontenay knew as yet that his daughter was having an affair. He must have thought that I had found out and was trying to get him to talk."

"What did he say?"

"After a moment he said in a hard voice:

" 'I don't know any Madame Josset.'

"So I told him that my paper would carry the news

the next day and would give all the details of the case. I added what I had just learned by telephone:

" 'One of the evening papers has the story of your meeting with your daughter and Adrien Josset on Rue Caulaincourt.' "

Maigret asked:

"Did you know him well?"

"As well as anyone in Fontenay did. I've seen him at the Préfecture and when he passed by in the street."

"Did he ever stop short while he was walking?"

"To look in the store windows, of course."

"Was he a sick man?"

"I don't know. He lived alone, didn't go to the café, and didn't talk much."

"Did you get the interview you wanted?"

"He kept on walking in silence. I asked him questions, whatever came into my head:

" 'Do you think Josset killed his wife?'

" 'Did he really mean to marry your daughter?'

"He scowled and didn't listen to me. Two or three times he growled:

" 'I have nothing to say.'

" 'But you did meet Adrien Josset?'

" 'I have nothing to say.'

"We reached the bridge. He turned left, along the quay, where he lives in a little brick house; a cleaning woman comes in daily. I took a picture of the house, since the paper never has enough pictures."

"Was the cleaning woman waiting for him?"

"No. She only worked for him in the morning."

"Who got his meals?"

"At lunch time he used to eat at the Trois Pigeons. He made his own dinner in the evening."

"And he didn't go out?"

"Hardly ever. Once a week to the movies."

"Alone?"

"Always."

"Did anyone hear anything that evening or during the night?"

"No. A cyclist going by at about one in the morning saw a light. When the cleaning woman came in that morning, the light was still burning."

Martin Duché had not undressed, nor had he eaten. Everything in the house was tidy.

As far as his actions could be reconstructed, he had taken a photograph album out of a drawer in the dining room. On the first pages there were yellowing portraits of his parents and wife; one of him as an artilleryman in the service; his wedding photograph; Annette a few months old, lying on a bearskin; then Annette at five, at ten, at her First Communion, and finally in a class group at the convent where she had been to school.

The album, open at that page, was lying on a little table by an armchair.

How long had Duché remained seated there before making his decision? He must have gone upstairs to his bedroom to take his revolver from the drawer in the bedside table. He had left the drawer open.

He had gone downstairs again, taken his seat in the armchair once more, and shot himself in the head.

The next morning the newspapers announced in banner headlines:

A SECOND VICTIM IN THE JOSSET CASE

In the minds of the readers, it was almost as if Josset had killed Annette's father with his own hands.

The papers spoke of the head clerk's life as a widower, dignified and lonely, of his love for his only daughter and of the shock he had received on reaching the apartment on Rue Caulaincourt and learning of his daughter's affair with her employer.

For Josset it meant almost certain conviction. Even Coméliau, who ought to have seen the facts from a purely professional point of view, became very excited when he spoke to Maigret on the telephone.

"Have you read about it?"

It was Thursday morning. The Inspector, who had just arrived in his office, had read the papers while standing on the bus platform.

"I hope that Josset has chosen a lawyer, since I intend to have him in my office this morning and speed the case up. The public wouldn't understand if we let things drag on."

That meant that Maigret had no more to do with it. The Magistrate was taking the case into his own hands, and theoretically from that point on the Inspector would only act under his instructions.

Perhaps he would never see Josset again except in court. And he would only know what the Magistrate saw fit to tell him about further interrogations.

It wasn't that day that he went to Niort and Fontenay, because Coméliau would certainly have heard about it and would have reprimanded him severely.

The rules forbade even the most innocent excursion outside Paris.

Even his first phone call to Doctor Liorant, who

lived on Rue Rabelais, Fontenay-le-Comte, and whom he had met previously in that town, was irregular.

"This is Maigret. Do you remember me, Doctor?"

The doctor answered coldly and carefully, and Maigret was immediately suspicious.

"May I, privately and personally, ask you for some information?"

"Go on."

"I wonder if Martin Duché was by any chance one of your patients."

There was a silence.

"I suppose it would not be a breach of professional etiquette . . ."

"He has consulted me."

"Did he suffer from a serious illness?"

"I am afraid I cannot answer that."

"One moment, Doctor. Forgive me if I press the matter. A man's life may depend on it. I have heard that Duché sometimes stood still suddenly, in the street or elsewhere, like a man suffering from angina pectoris."

"Did a doctor tell you that? If he did, he should not have done so."

"It was not a doctor."

"In that case it is only an unfounded assumption."

"Can't you tell me if he was threatened by sudden death?"

"I have nothing to say. I am sorry, Inspector, but I have several patients waiting to see me."

Maigret saw him again, with no more success, between trains on his journey to Niort and Fontenay, which he kept hidden from Coméliau and even Quai des Orfèvres.

Six

The Old Man Who
Couldn't Sleep

Rarely had spring been so lovely, and the newspapers vied with each other in announcing record
temperatures and record drought. Rarely, too, on
Quai des Orfèvres, had Maigret been seen so gloomy
and so irritable, to such an extent that those who
didn't know what it was all about inquired anxiously
after his wife's health.

Coméliau had taken the bit between his teeth,
enforcing the law to the very last letter, somehow
managing to keep Josset hidden away, so that the Inspector hadn't even the chance to speak a word to him.

Every day, or almost every day, the drug manufacturer was taken from the Santé prison to the Magistrate's office, where his lawyer, Maître Lenain, was
waiting for him.

He was a bad choice, and if Maigret had had the
chance he would have advised Josset against him.
Lenain was one of the three or four leading lights of
the bar, specializing in court trials attracting nation-
wide interest. As soon as he took over a spectacular
case, he occupied as much space in the newspapers
as any film star.

Reporters waited for his almost daily statements, his sarcastic comments, and, because of two or three acquittals that had been thought impossible, he was called the counsel for lost causes.

After these interrogations Maigret would get erratic orders from Coméliau, mostly without explanation: witnesses to hunt out, details to be checked, tasks even more irksome because they seemed to have little connection with the crime on Rue Lopert.

This was not done from personal animosity; if Coméliau had always distrusted the Inspector and his methods, it was due, rather, to the gulf separating their points of view.

It all came down to the question of social classes. The Magistrate had remained a man of an unchanging background in a changing world. His grandfather had presided over the highest Courts of Appeal, in Paris, and his father still sat on the Council of State, while one of his uncles was French Ambassador in Helsinki.

He himself had studied economics to enter the Superintendence of Finance, and it was only after failing the examination that he had taken up the law.

He was the typical product of his society, the slave of its ways, its rules of conduct, even its language.

One would have thought that his daily experiences in the Palais de Justice would have affected his concepts of human nature, but that was not so; he was invariably influenced by the point of view held by his class.

In his eyes Josset, if not a born criminal, was the guilty type. Had he not fraudulently entered a class which was not his own, first through a sinful affair, then through an ill-suited marriage? Didn't his affair with Annette and his promise to marry her confirm this opinion?

On the other hand, the young girl's father, Martin Duché, who had committed suicide rather than face dishonor, was a man after Coméliau's own heart. He was, according to popular belief, the model of the honest civil servant, humble and self-effacing, for whom nothing could soften the blow of his wife's death.

The fact that he had been drunk that evening on Rue Caulaincourt was of no importance to Coméliau, while that detail had great significance to the Inspector.

Maigret could have sworn that Annette's father had been ill for a long time, probably with an incurable disease.

And his dignity, wasn't it all really based on pride?

He had returned to Fontenay sick at heart, ashamed, in fact, of his behavior the previous evening, and, instead of finding peace and silence, he immediately ran into a journalist and a photographer on the station platform.

That worried Maigret, as did Doctor Liorant's attitude. He determined to come back to those points, to try to bring the matter into the open, even though his hands were tied.

His men had covered kilometers in Paris verifying facts, and Maigret had drawn up a timetable of Josset's actions on the night of the crime. He didn't know that this timetable would be of vital importance.

During the course of his only interrogation at Quai des Orfèvres, Josset had stated that he had wandered around after leaving Rue Caulaincourt at about 3:30, and that his first stop had been at a bar near Place de la République.

This bar, La Bonne Chope, had been found on Boulevard du Temple, and a waiter remembered him. Because of a customer who came every day on the stroke of nine and who had not yet arrived when Josset left, his visit to Boulevard du Temple could be fixed between a quarter to nine and nine o'clock.

That checked, then.

At the Select, on Avenue des Champs-Elysées, it was even easier, because Jean, the barman, had known the drug manufacturer for years.

"He came in at 9:20 and asked for a whiskey."

"Was that his usual drink?"

"No. He usually had a split of champagne. I had even reached for the bucket where we always keep some on ice when I saw him come in."

"Did anything about his manner strike you as odd?"

"He drank his whiskey in one gulp, held the glass out to be refilled, and instead of talking he stared straight ahead. I asked him:

" 'Not feeling well, Monsieur Josset?'

" 'Not so good.'

"He added something about some food that hadn't agreed with him, and I offered him some bicarbonate of soda.

"He refused and had a third whiskey before he went off, still very preoccupied."

That checked, too.

Still, according to Josset, he had then gone toward Rue Lopert, where he arrived at five past ten.

Torrence had questioned all the people living on

the street. Most houses had had their shutters closed
at that time. One of the neighbors had come home at
a quarter past ten and hadn't noticed anything odd.

"Were there any cars parked in front of Josset's
house?"

"I think so. A big one, anyway."

"And the little one?"

"I couldn't say."

"Did you see any lights on?"

"I think so. I couldn't swear to it."

Only the owner of the house across the street was
certain of what he had seen, so certain that Torrence
had repeated his questions three or four times and
had written down the answers word for word.

He was one François Lalinde, seventy-six years of
age, a colonial administrator retired some years before. Since he was not in the best of health—he
frequently came down with a fever—he never left the
house where he lived. He was cared for by a maid he
had brought back from Africa, whom he called Julie.

He stated that, according to his custom, he had not
gone to bed before four in the morning, and that he
had spent the first part of the night in his armchair by
the window.

He showed this armchair to Torrence. It was on
the second floor, in a room that was bedroom, li-
brary, living room, and curiosity shop all at once. It
was the only room in the house he really used, and
he rarely left it except to go to the bathroom next
door.

He was an impatient, easily angered man who
could not bear to be contradicted.

"Do you know your neighbors across the street?"

"By sight, sir, only by sight!"

He seemed to be sneering unpleasantly.

"Those people have chosen to live so that everyone can see them. They don't even have the decency to put shutters on the windows."

"Of whom are you speaking?"

"Both of them. The woman as well as the man. The servants aren't any better."

"Did you see Josset come home on Tuesday evening?"

"How would I not see him, since I was seated by the window?"

"Were you doing nothing but looking out onto the street?"

"I was reading. Every noise made me jump. I hate noises, particularly the noise of cars."

"Did you hear a car stop in front of the Jossets' house?"

"And I jumped, as usual. I consider noise to be a personal insult."

"So you heard Monsieur Josset's car, and probably the shutting of the car door?"

"I heard that, too, yes indeed, young man!"

"Did you look out?"

"I looked out and saw him going into the house."

"Were you wearing a wristwatch?"

"No. There is a clock on the wall, exactly opposite my chair, as you can see. It is never more than three minutes off a month."

"What time was it?"

"10:45."

Torrence, who had read Josset's statement, as had all Maigret's colleagues, pressed the point.

"Are you sure it wasn't 10:05?"

"Positive. I am a man of precision. I have been so all my life."

"Do you never fall asleep in your chair in the evening or at night?"

This time Monsieur Lalinde was angry, and poor Torrence had a hard time calming him down. The old man could not allow himself to be in the wrong, especially about his sleep, since he prided himself on not sleeping.

"Did you recognize Monsieur Josset?"

"Who else could it have been?"

"I am asking you if you recognized him?"

"Of course."

"Could you make out his features?"

"The street lamp isn't far away, and there was a moon."

"Were there any windows lit up at that time?"

"No, monsieur."

"Not even in the maid's room?"

"The maid had gone to bed half an hour before."

"How do you know?"

"Because I saw her shut her window, and her light went out immediately afterward."

"What time was that?"

"At a quarter past ten."

"Did Monsieur Josset put on the light on the ground floor?"

"He most certainly did."

"Do you remember seeing the ground floor lit up after he went in?"

"Perfectly."

"And then?"

"Then what always happened, happened. The ground floor was in darkness once more, and the lights went on on the second floor."

"In which room?"

Josset's bedroom and his wife's both looked out onto the street, Josset's on the right, Christine's on the left.

"In both."

"Did you see anything of what was going on in the house?"

"No. I wasn't interested."

"Can you see through the curtains?"

"Only a shadow when someone walks between the lights and the windows."

"So you didn't look even for a minute?"

"I went straight back to my book."

"Until when?"

"Until I heard a door across the street open and shut."

"When was that?"

"Twenty minutes past twelve."

"Did you hear a car engine?"

"No. The man went toward the church on foot. He was carrying a suitcase."

"Were there any lights still on in the house?"

"No."

After that, the last few hours tallied with the time-table Josset had given Maigret. And from then on there were plenty of witnesses. They had found the driver of the 403 from the taxi stand by the Auteuil church, Brugnali by name.

"I picked up the fare at 12:30. I noted the trip in

my book. He was carrying a suitcase, and I took him
to Avenue Marceau.''

''What was he like?''

''A real softy, reeking of liquor. I asked him
which station he wanted, because of the suitcase.''

On Avenue Marceau, Josset had paid the fare and
gone toward a large unattached building. It had a
brass plate to the left of the door.

They found the second taxi, too, the one Josset
had taken when he left the offices.

The night club he had visited at 1:30 was a small
place called Le Parc aux Cerfs. The doorman and the
bartender remembered him.

''He didn't want a table. He seemed surprised to
find himself in a place like this, and he seemed
embarrassed watching Ninouche doing her strip act
on the dance floor—Ninouche comes on at the end of
the first show, so I can fix the time. He drank a
whiskey and bought one for Marina, one of the host-
esses, but he didn't pay any attention to her.''

Meanwhile, outside, the taxi driver was having an
argument with another taxi driver. He worked in
league with the doorman and was trying to stop him
parking there.

'' 'Go and get your money, and I'll pick up your
fare when he comes out.' ''

Josset's arrival put an end to the argument, and the
taxi in which he had left his suitcase took him back
to Rue Lopert. Although he knew the neighborhood,
the driver took a wrong turn, and Josset had had to
set him right.

''It was 1:45, maybe 1:50, when I let him off.''

''What was he like?''

"Drunker than when he went in."

Lalinde, the former colonial administrator, confirmed the return. The lights had gone on again.

"On the ground floor?"

"Certainly. Then upstairs."

"In both rooms?"

"And in the bathroom, which has frosted glass windows."

"Did Josset go out again?"

"At 2:30, after he had put out all the lights."

"Did he take his car?"

"No. And this time he went toward Rue Chardon-Lagache, carrying a parcel."

"What size parcel?"

"Quite big, longer than it was wide."

"Twelve inches long? Fifteen?"

"I would say sixteen."

"And how wide?"

"About eight."

"Weren't you in bed?"

"No. At 3:48 exactly I heard a police siren and saw half a dozen policemen leap out onto the sidewalk and go into the house."

"So, if I've got it right, you didn't leave your chair either in the evening or at night."

"Only at half past four, to go to bed."

"Did you hear anything after that?"

"Cars coming and going."

Here, too, the times coincided, for Josset had reached the Auteuil Police Station at half past three, and the van had been sent to Rue Lopert a few moments afterward, when he was just beginning to make his statement.

Maigret had passed this report on to Coméliau. A little later the Magistrate asked him to come to his office, where he was sitting alone.

"Have you read it?"

"Of course."

"Has anything struck you?"

"One point. I'll tell you about it later."

"What strikes me is that Josset has told the truth about most things, those with no direct bearing on the crime. His timetable is correct for most of the night.

"But while he says he went in at 10:05 at the latest, Monsieur Lalinde saw him go in at 10:45.

"So he wasn't asleep in the hall, as he says he was, at that time.

"He went upstairs at 10:45 and put on the lights *in both rooms*.

"Note that the time corresponds with what Doctor Paul considers the probable time of the murder. What do you think?"

"I'd like to make a simple observation. According to Torrence, Monsieur Lalinde smoked very black cigars continuously throughout the interview, those little Italian cigars people call coffin nails."

"I don't see the connection."

"I expect he smokes at night, too, in his armchair. If that is so, he almost certainly finds he needs to drink."

"He could have everything within reach."

"Of course. He is seventy-six, according to the report."

The Magistrate still didn't understand.

"I wonder," Maigret continued, "if he didn't at

any time have to relieve his bladder. Old men generally . . .''

''He states that he did not leave his chair, and everything points to his being a man whose word can be trusted.''

''And he is an obstinate man who must be right whatever the cost.''

''Since he only knew Josset by sight he had no reason to . . .''

Maigret would have liked to see Monsieur Lalinde's doctor. It was the second time he had wanted to call on that type of witness.

''You are forgetting professional etiquette.''

''I am not forgetting it, unfortunately.''

''And you are forgetting that it is in Josset's interests to lie.''

Duché's suicide in Fontenay-le-Comte had definitely turned public opinion against Josset. The press had given it good coverage. They had printed photographs of Annette weeping as she boarded the train for Fontenay:

''Poor Papa! Had I known . . .''

They had interviewed employees at the Sous-Préfecture and shopkeepers of Fontenay-le-Comte, all of whom sang the head clerk's praises.

''A worthy man, with great integrity. Worn out by grief at his wife's death, he couldn't bear the disgrace . . .''

Maître Lenain answered the reporters' questions like a man preparing a crushing retort:

''Wait! The investigation is only in its early stages.''

''Do you have any new evidence?''

"I am keeping it for my good friend Maître Coméliau."

He named the day, the hour when all would be told, keeping their curiosity alive. When, as he himself said, he dropped the bomb, there were so many reporters and photographers in the corridors of the Palais de Justice that the police had to be called in to control them.

The "suspense" lasted three hours, during which four men were closeted in the Magistrate's chambers: Adrien Josset, who had been much photographed as he arrived; Maître Lenain, who had been no less popular; Coméliau; and his clerk of the court.

As for Maigret, he was attending to various administrative matters in his office on Quai des Orfèvres.

Two hours after the meeting, he was brought the newspapers. They all had more or less the same headline:

JOSSET ACCUSES!

The subheads were varied:

Josset, Cornered, Takes Offensive

And:

Defense Tries Desperate Maneuver

Coméliau, as usual, refused to make a statement and remained in his chambers.

Lenain, as usual, not only gave a written statement to the reporters but also held what was in fact a press conference in the corridors of the Palais de Justice immediately after his client had left accompanied by two policemen.

The statement was brief.

Up to now, Adrien Josset, who has been accused of the murder of his wife, has chivalrously kept silent on her private life and habits.

On the advice of counsel, he has finally decided that when his case is brought before the Grand Jury he will lift a corner of this veil of secrecy, and as a result of this the investigation will take a new turn.

It will be shown that many people could have killed Christine Josset. Little has been said of her until now, since people have been so busy condemning her husband.

Maigret would have liked to have known what had prompted this decision, to have known what was going on in the meetings that had taken place between lawyer and client in the cell in the Santé prison.

It reminded him somewhat of the scene on Rue Caulaincourt. Annette's father had come in, and all he had said was, "What are you planning to do?"

At once Josset, who hid behind Monsieur Jules when he had to fire an employee, had promised to divorce his wife and marry the girl.

Couldn't a clever and unscrupulous man like Lenain make Josset say anything he wanted?

Naturally the reporters had bombarded the lawyer with questions.

"Do you mean to say that Madame Josset had a lover?"

The barrister smiled mysteriously.

"No, gentlemen, not a lover."

"Lovers?"

"That's putting it too simply, and it wouldn't explain anything."

They didn't understand. He alone knew what he was getting at.

"Madame Josset, as was her privilege, remember, had protégés. Her friends will confirm this, and in some circles the protégés were spoken of as if they were racehorses belonging to some well-known owner."

Complacently he explained:

"When she was very young, she married a well-known man, Sir Austin Lowell, who formed her tastes and taught her the ways of the world—the world of power, of those who pull the strings. At first, like so many others, she was only an ornament.

"You must understand this: she was not Austin Lowell. She was the beautiful Lady Lowell, the woman he dressed and covered with jewels, showed off at the races, at opening nights, in night clubs and drawing rooms.

"When, at less than thirty years of age, she was widowed, she wanted to continue this style of life, but *on her own terms*, if I may put it that way.

"She did not wish to be the subsidiary part of a couple, the accessory or ornament, but the first.

"That is why, instead of marrying a man of her own class, which would have been easy for her, she sought out Josset, who was working in a drugstore.

"She in her turn needed to dominate, needed to have beside her someone who would owe her everything, who would be her property.

"Unfortunately it happened that the young pharmacist had a stronger personality than she had thought.

"He did so well in the drug manufacturing business that he became a person in his own right.

"That's all. Therein lies the drama.

"She was growing older and felt that the time when she would no longer be attractive to men would soon be upon her . . ."

"Excuse me," interrupted a journalist. "Did she have lovers before this?"

"Let us say that she had never lived according to the bourgeois moral code. The day came when she no longer dominated her husband, and so she looked for others to dominate.

"It is these whom I called her protégés, using the word she herself chose, and which it appears she uttered with a complacent smile.

"There were many of them. Only some are known. There were certainly others who are not known but whom I hope the investigation will uncover.

"For the most part they were unknown artists—painters, musicians, singers, whom she found God knows where and whom she determined to launch on their careers.

"I could name you one singer, very popular today, who owes his success solely to his chance encounter with Madame Josset, who met him in the garage where he worked as a mechanic.

"Although some succeeded, others proved to be without talent, and after a few weeks or a few months she dropped them.

"Need I add that these young men did not always become resigned to returning to obscurity?

"She had presented them to her friends as the future stars of the stage, painting, the screen. She had given them clothes and a good home. They had lived in her shadow, in her wake.

"Then, one day, they were nobodies again."

"Could you give us names?"

"I leave that to the Magistrate. I have given him a list of people among whom are certainly some fine young men. We do not accuse anyone. We say only that some people had reason to resent Christine Josset."

"Anyone in particular?"

"Obviously one must look at her most recent protégés."

Maigret had thought of that. From the first he had felt he should find out about the victim's private life and her circle of friends.

Until now he had come up against a wall. And again it was, as in dealing with Coméliau, a question of class, of caste almost.

Christine Josset had moved in a world even more limited than that of the Magistrate—a handful of people whose names were always in the papers, whose every word and deed was reported, about whom many strange news items were published but who were in fact hardly known at all by the general public.

Maigret had been only a detective when he had made a sally that was often repeated to newcomers to Quai des Orfèvres. Told to watch a banker—a man who was arrested several months later—he had said to his Chief:

"To understand how his mind works I must break-fast with financiers."

Has not each social class its own jargon, its taboos, its weaknesses?

When he asked, ''What's your opinion of Madame Josset?'' people invariably answered, ''Christine? What a fabulous woman'' (for in her circle she was not a Josset, she was Christine), ''a woman interested in everything, passionate, in love with life . . .''

''And her husband?''

''A nice guy.''

This was said more coldly, showing that, in spite of his commercial success, Josset had never been completely accepted by his wife's friends. He was tolerated, like the mistress or wife of a celebrity, and they said:

''After all, if she likes him . . .''

Coméliau would be furious. He would be even more so when he had read all the papers. He had made up a case that satisfied him, and the time was coming when he had to put it to the Grand Jury.

Now the investigation had to begin all over again. It wasn't possible to ignore Lenain's accusations, since he had taken care to give them as much publicity as possible.

It was no longer a matter of questioning concierges, taxi drivers, neighbors.

It was necessary to enter a new circle, to elicit confidences, names, to make up a list of these now notorious protégés, and it would obviously fall to Maigret to check their alibis.

''But,'' objected one reporter, ''Josset says he was asleep in the living room, in an armchair, after he got home at 10:05. A reliable witness who lives across the street says that he arrived home only at 10:45.''

"A witness can be mistaken in good faith," retorted the lawyer. "Monsieur Lalinde, for that is the man you are speaking of, no doubt did see a man enter the house at 10:45, while my client was asleep."

"Would that be the killer?"

"Probably."

"Could he have gotten past Josset without seeing him?"

"The living room was in darkness. The more I think of it the more certain I am that, at the time of the murder, there were not two but three cars parked in front of the house. I have checked the positions. I have not been in Monsieur Lalinde's house, since the maid was not very hospitable. Nevertheless I am sure that from the old man's window one can see the Cadillac and a car parked in front of it, *but not a car parked behind.* I have asked for this theory to be checked. If I am right, I am ready to swear that there were three cars there."

Madame Maigret was quite excited that evening. She had held out for a long time, but she finally became passionately interested in a case that everyone in town was talking about.

"Do you think Lenain was right to attack?"

"No."

"Is Josset innocent?"

He looked at her without seeing her.

"It's a fifty-fifty chance."

"Will he be convicted?"

"Probably, especially now."

"Can't you do anything?"

This time he merely shrugged his shoulders.

Seven

Monsieur Jules and
Madame Chairman

Maigret, powerless to intervene, watched a phenomenon which he had observed several times and which still surprised him. His old friend Lombras, head of the Municipal Police, responsible for public order, for all demonstrations, and for regulating crowds, used to swear that the whole city of Paris, like any private individual, could sometimes have a bad night and wake up in a foul mood, ready to jump at any opportunity to indulge it.

It happens like that in criminal cases. A coldblooded murder, revolting in detail, may pass unnoticed, the investigation and then the trial taking place with the public indifferent, if not exactly amenable.

Then, for some unknown reason, a quite ordinary crime raises public indignation.

There was no organized campaign. Those who purported to be in the know said there was no one pulling strings, no one mounting a campaign against Josset.

Certainly the newspapers had made much of the case and continued to do so, but newspapers only reflect opinion and give their readers what they want to read.

Why did Josset have the whole world against him from the first?

The twenty-one stab wounds had something to do with it. When a murderer loses his head and keeps on attacking a dead body, people talk of savagery; while a psychiatrist might see that as a sign of diminished responsibility, the general public sees it as an aggravating circumstance.

Of all the people in the case, Josset had immediately become the bad guy, the villain. Perhaps there was an explanation for that: from the newspaper articles, even those who had never seen him could sense that he was a weak man, a "softy," and mediocrity is not easily pardoned.

One doesn't forgive someone who denies what seems to be a fact—and as far as the world at large was concerned, Josset's guilt was a fact.

If he had confessed, if he had pleaded a moment of passion, of mental aberration, and had asked forgiveness contritely, most people would have been inclined to leniency.

He chose, however, to defy *logic* and *reason,* and that was like a slap in the face to the people's intelligence.

Ever since the Tuesday when he had questioned him, Maigret had known that it would be like that. Coméliau's reactions had been one indication of it. The first headlines and subheads in the afternoon newspapers had been another.

Since then, feelings against Josset had only increased, and it was rare to hear someone doubt his guilt or to find, if not excuses for him, extenuating circumstances at least.

Martin Duché's suicide had made matters worse, for the ex-pharmacist was now considered guilty not of one murder, but of two.

Finally his lawyer, Maître Lenain, had added fuel to the fire by his ill-timed statements and accusations.

In these circumstances it was difficult to question witnesses. The most honest of them, in all good faith, tended only to remember things that went against the prisoner.

In fact Josset was unlucky. Take the matter of the knife, for example. He had said in his statement that he had thrown it into the Seine from the middle of the Pont Mirabeau. Ever since Wednesday a diver had searched the muddy bottom for hours, watched by hundreds of idlers hanging over the parapet, while photographers and even television cameramen started taking pictures every time the big brass helmet appeared.

The diver came up empty-handed every time, and he continued his search the next day with no better results.

For those who know the bed of the Seine, this wasn't surprising. The current is strong against the piles of the bridge and creates undertows that can carry quite a heavy object a considerable distance.

In other parts the mud is thick, and rubbish of all kinds sinks deep into it.

Josset could not point out the exact place where he had been standing; in the state of mind he was supposed to have been in, this was only to be expected.

In the mind of the public, all this was proof that he

had lied. He was accused of having hidden the weapon somewhere else, for some unknown reason. It wasn't only a question of the dagger. Monsieur Lalinde, the ex–colonial administrator, whose word no one doubted and whom it would have been dangerous to call a somewhat crazy old man, had described a parcel *of some bulk,* whose dimensions were much greater than those of a Commando knife.

What could the package Josset carried off after the murder contain?

Even a discovery which at first seemed in the prisoner's favor and which the lawyer was careless enough to boast about too soon, turned against him in the end.

The Criminal Identity Division had taken several fingerprints from the house on Rue Lopert, which, because of its modern architecture, was now being called "the glass house." These fingerprints, once classified, had been compared with those of Josset, of his wife, of the two servants, and of an employee of the gas company who had been in to read the meter on Monday afternoon, some hours before the crime.

One set of prints remained unidentified. They were found on the banisters and, more thickly, in the victim's bedroom and in her husband's.

They were the prints of a man with a broad thumb marked with a small, round, easily identifiable scar.

When questioned, Madame Siran stated that neither Madame Josset nor her husband had had any visitors in the last few days and that, as far as she knew, no stranger had been up to the bedrooms.

Carlotta, who was still on duty in the evenings after the cook had left, confirmed this statement.

In the papers this became:

A MYSTERY VISITOR?

Naturally Maître Lenain made a great fuss about this discovery, which he made the starting point of an important line of defense.

According to him, Doctor Paul could have made an error of judgment. There was nothing, said the lawyer, to prevent the murder having taken place a little before ten, that is, before Josset's arrival.

Even if the police surgeon were right, one must not reject the hypothesis of a stranger entering the house while Josset, who had had a lot to drink, slept soundly in a chair in the unlighted living room.

Lenain had conducted an experiment on the spot, at the same time of night. He had taken up his position in the chair that Christine's husband had occupied, and six unsuspecting people were asked to pass through the room in the dark, one after the other, and to climb the stairs. Only two of them noticed that he was there.

To this it was objected that the moon was not in the same position as it had been on the night of the crime, and that the sky was overcast.

In any case, Lalinde's statement was unshaken, and he refused to alter a word of it.

It was Maigret who had a visit from the decorator. This man had just read the papers and, worried, had gone to Quai des Orfèvres to tell what he knew. He had worked regularly for the Jossets. It was he who, some years before, had put in new curtains and wall-paper. Some months ago he had changed some of the curtains, including those in Madame Josset's bed-room, which had just been refurnished.

"The servants seem to have forgotten my visit," he said. "They mentioned the gas man, but not me. Three days ago I went to Rue Lopert because Madame Josset had told me that the curtain cords had come loose. That often happens. So on Monday at about three I happened to be passing nearby and took the opportunity to call."

"Whom did you see?"

"Madame Siran opened the door. She didn't come upstairs with me because she hates stairs, and she knows I know the house."

"Were you alone?"

"Yes. I'd left my buddy on another job on Avenue de Versailles. The job only took a few minutes."

"Did you see the maid?"

"She came for a minute into the room where I was working, and I said hello to her."

Neither of the women had remembered the deco-rator when they had been questioned.

Maigret took the man to Criminal Identity. His fingerprints were taken, and they corresponded ex-actly to those of the mysterious visitor.

The next day it was again Maigret who received the anonymous letter that was to increase public anger—a sheet of paper torn from a school exercise book and folded in four, then slipped into a cheap envelope with some grease marks on it, as if the message had been written on a kitchen table.

The postmark was that of the Eighteenth Arrondissement, where Annette Duché lived.

"Inspector Maigret, who thinks he's so clever, should question a certain Hortense Malletier, on Rue Lepic, who is a filthy abortionist. She had a visit from the Duché girl and her lover three months ago."

The way things stood, the Inspector decided to take the letter himself to Coméliau.

"Read this."

The Magistrate read the letter twice.

"Have you checked?"

"I didn't want to do anything without your instructions."

"You'd better see this Hortense Malletier yourself. Is she in your records?"

Maigret had already looked up the Vice Squad's records.

"She was arrested once, ten years ago, but nothing could be proved."

The Malletier woman lived on the fourth floor of an old building near the Moulin de la Galette. She was over sixty and suffered from dropsy, so she wore bedroom slippers and couldn't move without a cane. There was a sickening smell in the apartment, and ten or twelve canaries flew around in a large cage by the window.

"What do the police want with me? I'm a poor old woman who doesn't want anything from anyone any more."

Gray hair, so thin that her scalp showed through, framed her pallid face.

Maigret began by showing her a photograph of Annette Duché.

"Do you recognize her?"

"Her picture's been in the papers enough!"

"Did she come here to see you about three months ago?"

"What would she do here? I haven't read the cards for a long time."

"Did you read the cards, too?"

"So? Everyone earns their living as best they can."

"She was pregnant, and after you saw her she wasn't any more."

"Who made up that story? It's a lie!"

Janvier, who was with his superior, searched the drawers and found nothing, as Maigret had expected.

"We must know the truth. She didn't come here alone. There was a man with her."

"It's been years since any man set foot in my apartment."

She stuck to her story. She knew the routine. The concierge of the building, when she was questioned, said she hadn't seen Annette or Josset.

"Doesn't Madame Malletier often have young girls to visit her?"

"Long ago, when she used to read the cards, she did, young and old, and even men, whom you wouldn't expect to believe in such things. But she hasn't done that for a long time now."

That could all have been foreseen. Annette's attitude, when she was summoned by Maigret to Quai des Orfèvres, was less so. The Inspector began with a blunt question:

"How long had you been pregnant when you went to Madame Malletier in the Rue Lepic?"

Didn't Annette know how to lie? Was she taken by

surprise? Didn't she realize what depended on her reply?

She blushed, looked around her as if for help and glanced nervously at Lapointe, who was once again taking everything down in shorthand.

"I suppose I must answer that?"

"It would be wise to do so."

"Two months."

"Who gave you the address on Rue Lepic?"

Maigret was annoyed without knowing why, possibly because he thought she gave in too quickly. The concierge had played the game. So had the old abortionist—naturally, for she had more reason.

"Adrien."

"So you told him you were pregnant, and he talked about an abortion?"

"It wasn't quite like that. I had been worried for about six weeks, and he kept on asking what was wrong with me. He even accused me of loving him less than before. One evening I asked him if he knew of a midwife or a doctor who would . . ."

"Didn't he object?"

"He was very upset. He said, *'Are you sure?'*

"I said yes, that it wouldn't be long before it showed, and I'd have to do something."

"Did he know Madame Malletier?"

"No, I don't think so. He begged me to wait a few days and not to do anything before he decided."

"Decided what?"

"I don't know."

Josset had no children by his wife. Had he been moved by the idea of Annette giving him a son or a daughter?

Maigret, for his own satisfaction, would have liked to ask him this question among others, but all the interrogations were now Coméliau's prerogative, and he didn't see things the same way.

"Do you think he was tempted to make you have the child?"

"I don't know."

"Did he say anything about it?"

"For a week he was very gentle, very attentive."

"Wasn't he usually gentle?"

"He was kind and loving, but it wasn't the same thing."

"Do you think he told his wife about that?"

She jumped.

"His wife!"

One would have said that she was afraid of Christine even when she was dead.

"He wouldn't have done that, surely."

"Why not?"

"I don't know. A man doesn't tell his wife that another woman is expecting his child."

"Was he afraid of her?"

"He didn't hide anything from her. When I advised him to be careful, not to be seen with me in certain restaurants, for example, he assured me that she knew all about it and that it didn't matter to her."

"Did you believe him?"

"Not entirely. I don't believe it's possible . . ."

"Did you ever meet Christine Josset?"

"Several times."

"Where?"

"In the office."

"Do you mean in her husband's office?"

"Yes. I worked there, too. When she came to Avenue Marceau . . ."

"Did she go there frequently?"

"Two or three times a month."

"To see her husband, to take him somewhere?"

"No. Mostly to see Monsieur Jules. She was chairman of the board."

"Did she take an active interest in the business?"

"Not exactly active. She kept up with things, though, saw the accounts, had certain procedures explained to her."

This was a side of Christine that no one had yet talked about.

"I suppose she was curious about you?"

"The first few times, yes. The very first time, she looked me up and down, from head to foot, shrugged her shoulders, and said to her husband, 'Not bad.' "

"So she knew already?"

"Adrien had told her."

"Did she never speak to you privately? Didn't you ever get the idea that she was afraid of you?"

"Of me? Why would she be afraid of me?"

"If her husband had told her you were expecting his child . . ."

"That would have been different, of course. But I would never have let him tell her. Not only because of her, but the others."

"Your fellow workers?"

"Everybody. And my father, too."

"What happened at the end of the week?"

"One morning in the office, before opening the mail, he whispered quickly:

" 'I have an address. We have an appointment there this evening.'

"That evening when we left the office, he didn't take me straight home to Rue Caulaincourt. He left the car on Boulevard de Clichy, as a precaution, and we walked to Rue Lepic."

"Weren't you tempted to change your mind?"

"The woman frightened me, but I'd made up my mind."

"What about him?"

"After a few minutes he went outside to wait for me."

Maigret had taken his report to Coméliau, as he had to. Had there been a leak from the Magistrate's office? Coméliau was not the sort of man to spread around information of that kind. Would Lenain, who had had to be told professionally, be less discreet? Publicity about this was not in his client's interests, and, in spite of his earlier faux pas, he wouldn't have done that.

It was more likely that the person who had written the anonymous letter, annoyed that nothing about it had been printed, had gone directly to the newspapers. They had carried out their own investigation.

Madame Malletier, still denying everything, had been arrested, and the case was once more on the front pages.

Coméliau had been obliged to charge the girl, too, but she was given bail.

JOSSET AND MISTRESS ACCUSED OF
SECOND CRIME

If Annette was spoken about, it was in tones of pity, all responsibility being placed on her lover.

One could feel a real wave of hate growing around him every day. Even those who had been his friends could only malign him and tried to minimize their friendship.

"I knew him, like everyone else. But I was really Christine's friend. What an amazing woman . . ."

Amazingly dynamic, yes indeed. But what else?

"He wasn't the man she needed."

When pressed, they were unable to say just what kind of man she did need. As far as could be made out, she had been created to live her own life with complete independence.

"For a while he was her great love. Everyone wondered why, because Josset has never been sexy—he was no Don Juan. Besides, he's a weakling."

It hadn't occurred to anyone that Christine might have crushed all life out of that weakling.

"Had she stopped loving him?"

"They lived apart more and more. Especially since he became infatuated with that typist."

"Did it upset her?"

"It's hard to know just what Christine felt. She kept her feelings to herself."

"Even about her lovers?"

They would look reproachfully at Maigret, as if he weren't playing the game.

"She liked to give young people a hand, didn't she?"

"She went to lots of art shows and things."

"She had her stable, so to speak, didn't she?"

"She may have helped a beginner."

"Can you give me an example?"

"It's difficult. She was tactful enough not to make much of it. I remember she helped a young painter, particularly by bringing her friends and some reporters she knew to his first exhibition."

"What was his name?"

"I don't remember it. I think he was Italian."

"Is that all?"

As each day went by, he met a more and more organized resistance.

After the bomb he had so heedlessly dropped, Maître Lenain, for his part, tried to draw up a list of the protégés he had sworn existed. Maigret knew that he had the help of a detective agency run by one of his own former detectives. They had a freer hand than Police Headquarters and didn't have Coméliau always on top of them.

In spite of that, he hadn't found anything clear-cut. He had called Maigret to tell him of one Daunard, a former hotel porter in Deauville who was now a singer in Saint-Germain-des-Prés.

Although he wasn't yet widely known, he was beginning to make a name for himself in the night clubs on the Right Bank, and he had an engagement in a music hall, the Bobino.

Maigret went to see him in his hotel room on Rue Ponthieu. He was a well-built young man, unpolished, the same aggressive type as some young American stars.

At two in the afternoon he opened the door, wearing crumpled pajamas. Of the woman curled up in the sheets, only the blond hair could be seen.

"Maigret, is it?"

He had been expecting this visit at any time. He lit a cigarette and began to act like a film tough.

"I could forbid you to come in unless you have a warrant. Do you?"

"No."

Maigret was not prepared to discuss the legality of his visit.

"I warn you now I have nothing to say."

"Did you know Christine Josset?"

"So what? There are thousands of people in Paris who did."

"Did you know her intimately?"

"In the first place, that's none of your business. In the second, if you look hard enough you'll find several dozen men who've slept with her. And when I say dozens . . ."

"When did you last see her?"

"About a year ago. And if you're going to say that she gave me my start, you've got it wrong. The owner of a club in Saint-Germain had seen me in Deauville and given me his card, asking me to come to Paris to see him."

The woman in the bed pulled the sheet back a few inches and risked a one-eyed look.

"Don't worry, honey! I've got nothing to fear from these gentlemen. I can prove that I was in Marseilles the night Madame Christine was bumped off. They'll even find my name in big print on the program at the Miramar."

"Did you know any others?"

"Other whats?"

"Other friends of Madame Josset's."

"Do you think we were a club, maybe, or a guild? Then why didn't we wear a badge, eh?"

He was very pleased with himself. His girlfriend, still wrapped in the sheet, was doubled up with laughter.

"Is that all you want? Then, with your permission, I have better things to do. Right, honey?"

There were obviously others, the same type or different, who evidently didn't want to make themselves known. The painter who had been mentioned now lived in Brittany, where he painted seascapes, and there was nothing to show that he had been in Paris at the time.

A different kind of investigation, among the taxi drivers, hadn't brought any results either. Still, even after quite a long time, it's rare not to find the driver who has made a particular trip.

Several detectives had divided the companies, the taxi stands, and the owner cabs among them.

Each one was asked if he had taken anyone to Rue Lopert on the night of the crime. That brought no results. All they learned was that a couple who lived three doors away from the Jossets had come back from the theater by taxi a little before midnight.

Neither the driver nor the couple could remember if there had been any lights on in the glass house at that hour.

However, the fact that a taxi had stopped in the street at that time had one advantage: the former colonial administrator, who had said that not a thing of what went on in the street had escaped him, hadn't mentioned the vehicle. And yet the taxi had been parked there, engine running, for three or four minutes, because the customer, who had had no change, had gone into the house to get some.

A photograph of Martin Duché had been shown to thousands of drivers, particularly those who had their usual stands in the Caulaincourt area.

They had all seen it in the papers already. According to Annette, her father had left her about 9:30 that evening. He appeared not to have gotten back to his hotel by Gare d'Austerlitz before midnight, and the night watchman didn't remember seeing him come in.

What had the head clerk from Fontenay-le-Comte been doing all that time?

It appeared to be a complete blank. No driver remembered picking him up, although his figure and his face were easily recognizable.

Annette had admitted that he was not in his normal state of mind—although he was a total abstainer, he had had a considerable quantity to drink.

Even though it had had a calm enough ending, the scene on Rue Caulaincourt must nevertheless have upset him.

The fact remained that no taxi appeared to have taken him to Rue Lopert or anywhere else.

He had not been seen in the Métro station either, which, given the number of people passing through, didn't prove a thing.

And there were still the buses, in which he could have traveled completely unnoticed.

Was he the type of man to sneak stealthily into the Jossets' house? Would he not have rung the doorbell? Had he found the door open?

And how was it possible that, since he didn't know

the place, he could have crossed the living room in the dark and climbed the stairs to Christine's bedroom?

The murderer, if he wasn't the husband, wore gloves. He had either brought with him a fairly heavy weapon with which to inflict the wounds described by Doctor Paul, or he had used the Commando dagger that was in Adrien's bedroom.

Who, apart from close friends, could have known that that dagger was there? Moreover, it had to be admitted that, having committed the crime, the unknown man cleaned the weapon and left no trace whatsoever on a cloth, since the drug manufacturer had not seen any blood on the dagger.

The public was aware of these contradictions, for the journalists exercised their ingenuity by going in detail into every imaginable hypothesis. One of them had even printed the arguments for and against in parallel columns.

Maigret went to Avenue Marceau for the first time, to the mansion built at the end of the last century and now converted into offices.

Apart from the switchboards and a little room where visitors left their cards and filled out forms, the ground floor, with its paneling and its overdecorated ceilings, was only used for exhibition purposes.

The products of Josset & Virieu were displayed in glass cases, and there were also, sumptuously framed, diagrams and doctors' testimonials. And on huge oak tables lay the various medical publications that helped to sell the firm's products.

This time it was Monsieur Jules whom Maigret had come to see. He had already learned that Jules was not his first name but his surname, so he was not called that as a mark of familiarity.

The bright, almost bare room where two secretaries were working separated his office from Josset's, which was the largest in the building and had tall windows looking out over the trees in the avenue.

Monsieur Jules was sixty-five, with bushy eyebrows and dark hairs sprouting out of his nose and his ears. He reminded Maigret of Martin Duché, but was less subservient. Like him he typified the image usually brought to mind by the words ''honest servant.''

Actually, he had been in the firm long before Josset, indeed from the time of Virieu's father, and although his official title was head of personnel, he had the right to supervise everything else.

Maigret wanted to talk to him of Christine.

''Don't put yourself to any trouble, Monsieur Jules. I'm only passing by, and I am really not too sure what I ought to ask you. By chance I learned that Madame Josset was chairman of your board of directors.''

''That's right.''

''Was this only an honorary title, or did she take an active interest in the firm's business?''

He could already sense the unwillingness to speak that he was finding everywhere. Was it not precisely to avoid this that it is so important to act quickly in a criminal investigation? Madame Maigret knew this better than anyone, since she saw her husband come home so often in the early hours of the morning, if indeed he hadn't spent several nights on the job.

When people read newspapers they soon form an

opinion, and even when they believe themselves to be sincere and truthful, they tend to distort the truth.

"She took genuine interest in the business, in which, moreover, she had a considerable financial stake."

"A third of the registered capital, I believe?"

"A third of the shares, yes, another third belonging to Monsieur Virieu and the remaining third, for the past few years, to her husband."

"I understand that she came to see you two or three times a month."

"It was not quite as regular as that. She came from time to time, not only to see me but also to see the managing director and, sometimes, the chief accountant."

"Did she know what was what?"

"She had a very good business sense. She played the stock market with her own money, and I may say that she made a handsome profit from it."

"In your opinion, did she distrust the way her husband ran things?"

"Not only her husband. Everyone."

"Didn't this attitude make enemies for her?"

"Everyone has enemies."

"Did she have enemies in this firm? Did she ever take action against anyone in particular?"

Monsieur Jules scratched his nose, a malicious gleam in his eye, not in the least embarrassed, but he hesitated a little before speaking.

"Have you studied the management and the personnel of a big business firm before, Inspector? As long as there are enough interested parties, and as long as departments are in more or less open competition, there are bound to be cliques.''

It was true even of Quai des Orfèvres, as Maigret knew only too well.

''Were there cliques in this firm?''

''There probably still are.''

''May I ask to which you belong?''

Monsieur Jules frowned, grew more serious, and stared at his pigskin desk set.

''I was quite devoted to Madame Josset,'' he said finally, weighing his words.

''And to her husband?''

At that, Monsieur Jules got up to reassure himself that there was no one listening behind the door.

Eight

Madame Maigret's Coq au Vin

It was the Maigrets' turn to have their friends the Pardons to dinner on Boulevard Richard-Lenoir. Madame Maigret had spent all day cooking amid a veritable symphony of noises, for the season of wide-open windows had begun, and the life of Paris swept into apartments with the warm breezes.

Alice had not come, and it was her mother's turn to listen for the telephone, since they were waiting to hear at any moment that the young woman had been rushed off to the hospital for the delivery.

When dinner was over, the table cleared, and coffee served, Maigret offered the doctor a cigar while the two women began to whisper in a corner. Among other things Madame Pardon could be heard to say:

"I've always wondered how you make it."

They were talking about the coq au vin that had been the main dish at dinner. Madame Pardon continued:

"There's a faint taste of something, hardly noticeable, that makes all the difference, and I can't decide what it is."

"But it's quite simple really—I suppose you add a glass of cognac at the last moment?"

"Cognac or armagnac, whichever I have at hand."

"Well, although it's not orthodox, I put in a little Alsatian plum brandy. That's all there is to it."

All during dinner Maigret had been in a very good mood.

"Have you been very busy these days?" Pardon asked.

"Very busy indeed."

It was true, but it was amusing work.

"I'm living in the midst of a circus!"

For some time now there had been a series of burglaries carried out in such a way that the perpetrator could only be a professional acrobat, probably a contortionist of either sex, so that Maigret and his colleagues spent the entire day among people of the circus and the music halls, and the oddest people showed up on Quai des Orfèvres.

They were dealing with a newcomer who used new methods, which is much rarer than one might think. Everything had to be learned afresh, and a peculiar excitement pervaded the Crime Squad.

"Last month you didn't have time to tell me the end of the Josset case," murmured Doctor Pardon, once he was settled in his armchair with a drink in his hand.

He never had more than one glass, but he swallowed it in tiny sips that he held on his tongue, the better to savor the bouquet.

A different expression crossed the Inspector's face when he thought of the crime on Rue Lopert.

"I don't remember now exactly how far I got.

From the beginning I had guessed that Coméliau wouldn't let me see Josset again, and that is exactly what happened. He held on to him so tightly that one might have thought he was jealous of him.

"The preliminary investigation took place inside his chambers, so that we on Quai des Orfèvres knew no more about it than what we could read in the papers.

"For nearly two months, ten of my men, sometimes more, engaged in depressing inquiries.

"Our investigation was carried out on several levels at once. First there was the purely technical side, the reconstruction of each person's timetable on the night of the crime, the searching, twenty times over, of the house on Rue Lopert, where we kept hoping to find a clue that had previously escaped our notice, including the notorious Commando knife.

"I myself questioned the two servants, the tradesmen, and the neighbors heaven knows how many times. And to complicate matters there was the flood of letters, both anonymous and signed, mostly signed, which couldn't be ignored.

"That is inevitable when a case takes hold of the public's imagination.

"Madmen, crackpots, people who have had it in for their neighbors for years, or just people who think they know something, they all come to the police, and we have to separate the true from the false.

"I went to Fontenay in secret, almost illegally, without any result, as I think I told you.

"You see, Pardon, once a crime has been committed, nothing is simple any more. The deeds and words of ten or twenty people, which a few hours earlier seemed so natural, are suddenly seen in a more or less incriminating light.

"Everything is possible!

"There is no theory that is in itself ridiculous. Nor is there an infallible way of being sure of a witness's good faith or his memory.

"The public makes up its mind by instinct, prompted by sentimental considerations and elementary logic.

"But *we* have to doubt everything, to look everywhere, not to leave any theory untested.

"So, on the one hand, Rue Lopert; on the other, Avenue Marceau.

"I didn't know anything about the drug business, and, in order to do my job, I had to learn how this one, which, together with its laboratories, employed more than three hundred people, was run.

"How could I, in a few interviews, see how Monsieur Jules's mind worked?

"He wasn't the only one who played an important part on Avenue Marceau. There was Virieu, the founder's son; then there were the heads of various departments, the technical advisers, doctors, pharmacists, chemists . . .

"This world was divided into two main camps that could roughly be called the old guard and the new, the former considering that only drugs sold on prescription should be made there, the latter preferring products allowing a high profit margin, drugs that can be launched with publicity campaigns in the papers and by radio."

Pardon murmured:

"I know a little about that."

"It seems that Josset basically inclined to the old

guard, but he let himself be pushed, under pressure, into the second group.

"Still, he did resist."

"And his wife?"

"She was the leader of the vanguard. She had been instrumental in the dismissal of an advertising director two months before. He had been a good man with excellent connections in the medical world, an avowed enemy of cheap drugs.

"Both on Avenue Marceau and at Saint-Mandé that made for an undercurrent of intrigue, suspicion, and probably hatred. But that didn't get me anywhere.

"We couldn't dig deeply into everything at once. Normal day-to-day work takes up the time of most of the men even when a sensational case breaks.

"I have rarely felt our shortcomings so much. At a time when we needed to know the life history of ten, maybe even thirty people who hadn't even been heard of the previous day, I only had a handful of men at my disposal.

"They are expected to penetrate worlds they don't know and to form an opinion in a ridiculously short time.

"Now, in a trial, the word of a witness, a concierge, a taxi driver, a neighbor, a chance passer-by, can have more weight than the denials and statements made under oath by the accused.

"Adrien Josset kept on denying everything, in spite of stronger and stronger evidence. His lawyer kept on making unfortunate statements to the press.

"I had fifty-three anonymous letters that led us to every part of Paris and the suburbs, and we had, besides, to ask forces in the provinces to collect evidence.

"Some people believed they had seen Martin Duché in Auteuil that night, and there was even a tramp near the Pont Mirabeau who claimed that Annette's father, blind drunk, had propositioned him.

"Others told us the names of young men who had been Christine Josset's protégés.

"We followed up every lead, even the most unlikely, and I sent a fresh report to Coméliau every evening. He would read it and shrug his shoulders.

"One of the young men brought to our notice in this way was named Popaul. The anonymous letter said:

" 'You will find him at the Bar de la Lune on Rue de Charonne. Everyone there knows him, but they won't say anything because they've all got something to hide.'

"The author gave details and said that Christine Josset liked slumming and that she had met Popaul several times in a boarding house near the Saint-Martin Canal.

" 'She bought him a little car, a *quatre-chevaux*. That didn't stop Popaul beating her up more than once and making her scream.' "

Maigret himself went to Rue de Charonne, and the bar in question was indeed a meeting place for young delinquents, who vanished when he appeared. He questioned the landlord and the barmaid and, in the days following, regular customers, whom he had some difficulty in finding.

"Popaul? Who's that?"

They said that too innocently. If one were to believe them, no one had ever heard of Popaul, and the Inspector could get no more satisfaction in the boarding houses near the canal.

From the motor vehicles bureau he could get no useful information. Several owners of new *quatre-chevaux* were named Paul. They had even found some of them, but four or five had left Paris.

As for Christine's friends of both sexes, they kept the same polite silence. Christine was a charming woman, a "darling," a "pet," an "exceptional woman."

Madame Maigret had taken Madame Pardon into the kitchen to show her something, and then, so as to leave the men in peace, the two women settled down in the dining room. Maigret had taken off his jacket, and was smoking a meerschaum pipe that he used only at home.

"The Grand Jury was named, and we at the Quai were effectively put out of commission. Other cases kept us busy all summer. The papers announced that Josset, suffering from nervous depression, had been moved to the infirmary at the Santé, where he was being treated for a stomach ulcer.

"Some people sneered, because it has become almost a tradition for persons of a certain class to pretend that they are ill when they are put in prison.

"When, after the summer recess, he was seen at the trial, in the dock, you could see that he had lost more than forty pounds and that he was a changed man. His clothes hung loosely on his emaciated body, his eyes were sunken, and, although his counsel challenged the public and the witnesses with his manner, he himself seemed indifferent to what was going on around him.

"I didn't hear the Judge's questioning of the accused, or the statements of Coméliau and the Inspector of the Auteuil police, who were the first witnesses, because I was in the witnesses' waiting room. Among others, I was rubbing shoulders with the concierge from Rue Caulaincourt, who was wearing a red hat and seemed very pleased with herself, and with Monsieur Lalinde, the former colonial administrator, whose testimony was the most damaging and who seemed to be in a very bad state. I thought he, too, had grown thinner. He seemed to be in the grip of an obsession, and I wondered if he was going to change his original statement in public.

"Whether I liked it or not, I had to add my brick to the case so carefully built up by the prosecution.

"I was only an instrument. I could only say what I had seen, what I had heard, and no one asked me what I thought.

"I spent the remainder of the two days in court, and Lalinde didn't retract; he didn't change one word of his previous statement.

"As I walked along the corridors during adjournments, I heard what the public thought, and it was obvious that not a soul doubted Josset's guilt.

"Annette, too, appeared on the witness stand, causing a disturbance in court, with whole rows of people standing up to see her. The judge threatened to clear the court.

"She was asked detailed questions—leading questions, really, particularly about the abortion.

" 'Was it indeed Josset who took you to see Madame Malletier on Rue Lepic?'

" 'Yes, sir.'

" 'Face the jury, please.'

"She wanted to add something else, but they were already asking her the next question."

Several times Maigret had the impression that she was trying to explain details that no one was worrying about. For example, hadn't it been she who, when she told her lover that she was pregnant, had asked him if he knew an abortionist?

"It went on like that," the Inspector said to Pardon.

Sitting in the public gallery, he could hardly keep still. He continually wanted to raise his hand, to interrupt.

"In two days, in barely a dozen hours, including the reading of the charge, the case for the prosecution, and the case for the defense, they had tried to sum up, for people who had known nothing about it before, a whole way of life—to describe not only one character but several, since Christine, Annette, her father, and others who came into the case marginally were brought into it one by one.

"It was hot in the courtroom, for that year we were having a wonderful Indian summer. Josset kept looking at me. Several times I caught his eye, but it was only at the end of the first day that he seemed to recognize me and smiled slightly in my direction.

"Had he understood that I had doubts, that this case left me feeling uncomfortable, that I was annoyed with myself and with others, and that because of him I had come to hate my profession?

"I don't know. Most of the time he was sunk in a kind of indifference that several reporters took to be scorn. Since he had taken care with his appearance, they spoke of his vanity and tried to find proof of it in his career and even in his childhood and youth.

"The Attorney General, who was himself acting as Public Prosecutor, also stressed this vanity:

" 'A vain weakling . . .'

"Maître Lenain's aggressive remarks didn't change the atmosphere in the court—quite the opposite!

"When the jury retired, I was sure what their answer to the first questions would be: 'yes,' and probably unanimously—

"Josset had killed his wife.

"I expected, in all fairness, a 'no' to the second question, which was about premeditation. As for extenuating circumstances . . .

"Some people were eating sandwiches, there were women passing sweets around, the reporters had calculated that they had time to run to the bar in the Palais de Justice for a drink.

"It was late when the foreman of the jury, a hardware dealer from the Sixth Arrondissement, was called upon to speak. He held a slip of paper in his trembling hand.

" 'To the first question: yes.

" 'To the second question: yes.

" 'To the third question: no.'

"Josset had been found guilty of killing his wife, of having done so with premeditation, and he was not allowed the benefit of extenuating circumstances.

"I saw him take the blow. He grew pale, he was shocked, he couldn't believe his ears at first. He began to wave his arms as if struggling, then he suddenly grew calm and, directing one of the most tragic looks I have ever seen toward the public gallery, he said in a clear voice:

" 'I am innocent!'

"There were some jeers. A woman fainted. Police rushed into the courtroom.

"In no time at all, Josset had been whisked away, and a month later the press announced that the President of the Republic had turned down his appeal.

"No one thought about him any more. A new trial captured people's imaginations, a case with salacious disclosures in quick succession, so that Josset's execution only took up a few lines on the fifth page of most papers."

There was silence. Pardon stubbed out his cigar in the ashtray while the Inspector filled his pipe again. The women were still talking in the next room.

"Do you think he was innocent?"

"Twenty years ago, when I was a newcomer to the profession, I would perhaps have said 'yes' without hesitating. Since then I've learned that anything, even the improbable, is possible.

"Two years after the trial, I had in my office a tough customer suspected of involvement in the white slave trade. It wasn't the first time we had seen him. He was part of our regular clientele.

"His identity card classified him as a sailor, and in fact he did a lot of commuting to South and Central America on cargo boats, though he spent most of his time in Paris.

"With that kind of person things are different, since we're on familiar ground.

"And sometimes we can work out a compromise.

"At one point, looking at me out of the corner of his eye, he muttered:

" 'Suppose I had something to sell?'

" 'What then?'

" 'Some information you'd be very interested in.'

" 'What about?'

" 'The Josset case.'

" 'That's been over for a long time.'

" 'That's no reason not to . . .'

"In exchange, he wanted me to keep his girlfriend out of it. He really seemed to be in love with her. I promised to go easy on her.

" 'On my last trip I met a guy called Popaul. A character who used to hang out in the Bastille district.'

" 'On Rue de Charonne?'

" 'Could be. He hadn't been doing very well over there, and I bought him a few drinks. About three or four in the morning, when he'd had half a bottle of tequila and was good and drunk, he began to talk:

" ' "The bosses here don't think I'm tough. They don't believe me when I tell them I chopped up a woman in Paris. Even less when I tell them she was a rich woman and nuts about me. But it's true, and I'll always be sorry I did such a mad thing. But I never could stand being treated in a certain way, and it was her fault for going too far. Haven't you ever heard of the Josset case?" ' "

Maigret stopped speaking. He took his pipe out of his mouth.

"My man couldn't tell me any more. Popaul, if that was his name—some people have wild imaginations—went on drinking and fell asleep. The next day he said he didn't remember a thing.''

"Didn't you go to the Venezuelan police?"

"Unofficially, since you had to watch your step. There are several Frenchmen over there who have good reason not to come back to France, some former convicts among them. In answer to my question, I got an official letter asking me to give more details concerning identity.

"Is there any such person as Popaul? Was he, proud of his virility and his toughness, angry at being treated by Christine Josset in the way that men treat a prostitute, and did he take his revenge on her?

"I have no way of knowing.''

He got up and stood in front of the window, as if to clear his mind.

While Pardon kept an eye on the telephone out of habit, Maigret asked him, a little later:

"By the way, what happened to the Polish tailor's family?"

It was the doctor's turn to shrug his shoulders.

"Three days ago I was called in to the Rue Popincourt because one of the children has measles. I found a North African there, living with the mother. She looked a bit embarrassed and said:

" 'It's for the children's sake, you see.' ''